WOMEN

& CHILDREN FIRST

Stories by
Bill Oliver

Mid-List Press
Minneapolis

Some of the stories in this collection originally appeared in the following
publications: *Carolina Quarterly*, "Ether"; *Cimarron Review*, "Conflicting
Forecasts"; *Descant*, "In Roger's Garden"; *Florida Review*, "Vigil"; *Indiana
Review*, "Loose Change"; *Kansas Quarterly*, "A State of Disrepair"; *Virginia
Quarterly Review*, "Companion."

These stories are works of fiction. Names, characters, places, and incidents
either are the product of the author's imagination or are used fictitiously, and
any resemblance to actual persons, living or dead, events, or locales is entirely
coincidental.

Library of Congress Cataloging-in-Publication Data
Oliver, Bill, 1949–
Women & children first : stories / by Bill Oliver
p.   cm. — "First series : short fiction"—Cover.
I. Title.
ISBN 0-922811-35-0 (pbk. : alk. paper)
PS3565.L4578W66   1998
813'.54 — dc21   97-44887   CIP

Manufactured in the United States

First printing: January 1998
01 00 99 98   5 4 3 2 1

♾ The paper used in this publication meets the minimum requirements of
the American National Standard for Information Sciences—Permanence of
Paper for Printed Library Materials, ANSI Z39.48–1984.

For Elizabeth

CONTENTS

IN ROGER'S
GARDEN

t comes to Martha on her hands and knees, the certain knowledge the earth she's scratching will have him soon. She lifts the clawed tool above her head, brings it down hard, and is once again surprised and angered by how little "give" there is to this dirt. As if her husband had not been coaxing flowers from it every spring and summer for more than thirty years. She looks up at Roger's bedroom window, its white shade drawn—a barrier as unyielding as this ground.

He wants her out here. It's his idea she should bring in the garden. "There's no one else," he told her. Already it was April. "If you don't get started," he said, "we'll miss the season altogether." He doesn't mention that when the season comes he won't be around to see it.

Roger was always thin enough to make her look dowdy by comparison. Clothes just hung on him. Now his body barely ripples the sheets. He looks like some magic trick lying there—the disappearing man, only his head and arms visible. Soon there will be nothing left. When Martha trims his hair—it is still the color of honey, with scarcely a speck of gray—she saves the clippings, hiding them inside her pillowcase.

He pretends to be unimpressed by what's happening to him and will not refer in any way to his rapidly vanishing person. With the doctor, a music lover like himself, he speaks only of classical records and stereo equipment. With her, it's the garden: "I think we should try spider grass for a border."

Something in her cries out for a proper reckoning, a squaring of accounts. A good and substantial man shouldn't be allowed to give everybody the slip like this. She's mentioned to him the possibility of a visit from Father Naro. He didn't say no. Not that she has any confidence in the priest's ability to reach him. She's counting on God, Who, she reminds herself, can make of any creature, even Theodore J. Naro, a worthy vessel. At least that's what she used to tell her husband and daughter when they mocked Naro's incoherent and sometimes sentimental homilies. Roger had finally shut her up on the subject of worthy vessels. "I'm sorry, dear," he said, "but when I try to picture our man of God as a vessel, all I see is a large Ball jar filled with applesauce." It must be a terrible burden, Martha thinks, to be so clever, to imagine there's always a smart answer for everything.

She strikes the ground again with the garden claw, and the pain which is constantly in her hand shoots all the way up to her shoulder. If not for the pain and awkwardness, she would find the arthritic condition of her hands grimly amusing. Like the tool she's using, the hands resemble a witch's claws. They would be good for scaring grandchildren. She used to play "Witch" with her daughter, Nancy, when she was little, chasing her around the house, threatening to put her in the oven. Roger would always dash in and rescue the child, banish the witch, send her howling back to nearby House Mountain where she belonged. Martha never minded playing the hag. They'd all been primed for their parts by the stories Roger told about the dark mountain visible from their yard on clear days, the exclusive dwelling place, he claimed, of all the wicked things for miles around. The stories had been scary but also reassuring since no witch, however determined, could do permanent harm to any member of a happy family. The invention of this safety clause was typical of Roger, who drew a protective circle around those he loved.

Their daughter is on Martha's mind a lot these days. Not the grown woman they never see anymore, but the bright, earnest little girl in plaid jumper and tennis shoes who had wanted more than anything to please people, and most of all her father. Martha wonders if the memory of their little girl comes to Roger, too. God knows, there's nothing else to sustain him, except the promise of this garden. Though the garden, she suspects, is only an excuse to keep her at bay.

WHEN ROGER WAS still bothering to weigh himself, with her help, Martha would sometimes read aloud the declining numbers. "One-four-two." "One-three-nine." "One-three-five." They alarmed her so much she couldn't bear merely to note them in silence.

"Don't you think we should tell Nancy?" Martha said.

"Absolutely not. I mean it, Martha." He hadn't been on speaking terms with their daughter for some time.

Martha lit a candle in church, praying the cancer would stop devouring him. But she's not pious; her mind wanders at Mass, and she doubts her faith is pure enough to make candles perform miracles. So she visited the library, read about the healing power of herbs, tried mixing star-in-the-earth with his food. Still the pounds fell from him.

She scolded him: "It's not very considerate, you know, weighing less than your wife."

"It's all right," he said, "as long as I'm taller than you."

She supposes it's an admirable thing, his fending off death like this. If only he didn't fend her off in the process. That protective circle of his, if it still exists, must be very small these days, with barely room for one.

Time is dwindling, faster than the numbers on his scales. He must feel it, too, though he only speaks of it in terms of what's left to do in the garden. Maybe he's very wise, keeping them both preoccupied with planting schedules. But to Martha it feels like such a waste of time, her enforced exile among the lilacs and hydrangea, while her husband fades from sight in the darkened room upstairs.

He suggested she hire a nurse, presumably to leave her more time in the garden. But on that point Martha was stubborn; she would provide whatever nursing he needed. He's needed remarkably little as it turns out. If not for the drugs, which keep him reasonably comfortable, she believes things might be different between them, though she feels guilty wishing more pain on him.

He had a bad dream while napping the other day. There was a moving van backed up to their front door.

"Where was it taking us?" Martha asks him.

"I don't know, but you were sitting at the wheel with the motor running."

"I suppose you were dragging your feet as usual."

"I couldn't find something I needed. The last thing you said was, 'I know where the button for the air horn on this thing is and if you don't come on I'm going to push it.'"

Martha wonders how she got to be the heavy in all this. Is it possible that somewhere along the line she turned into the hag she only used to impersonate? Maybe that's what he thinks, too, sensing in her anxious presence his personal angel of death. She's tried being more cheerful around him, but she's never shared his light, bantering touch with people, especially with the people she loves. Alone in the room with him, she feels positively leaden, while it's not hard to picture him floating up from the bed and drifting out a window, escaping to his garden, leaving her to pursue him along those winding paths she trudges daily.

She read an article in the oncologist's waiting room a few weeks ago that made her cry. It was humiliating, gasping and shedding tears over a silly magazine, surrounded by strangers with problems at least as bad as hers. The little receptionist who wears a diamond engagement ring and smells of bubble gum asked Martha if she'd like to lie down in one of the examining rooms, but she shook her head, went out to the car, and finished the article there. The writer had interviewed a famous psychologist who said it was impossible, in the end, to love someone you can't make happy. Martha wept because she knew the psychologist was a fool. What he claimed was impossible she had been doing all these years. Then she thought, so who's the bigger fool?

IT ISN'T TRUE she never made him happy. For one thing, she gave him Nancy. What pals the two of them were. As Martha stands at her kitchen sink and looks out the window, she can picture them in the garden even now, kneeling side by side, the sun on their blond heads, their hands plunged in dirt up to their wrists. Recently the memory has begun to change before her eyes; it seems to Martha the figures in the garden aren't kneeling but crouching, as if the earth has slipped a gear, started spinning faster, and they must try to hold on. It makes her dizzy and a little sick to her stomach. She has to shut her eyes, put her palms flat on the Formica counter, until the spell passes.

Nancy stayed home longer than other children, enrolling at the local college. She made them proud, earned high grades; Nancy was smart. Martha guessed it was ambition she lacked. Following a brief, unhappy stint in graduate school, she came back to them, reclaiming the rose-colored room with the canopied bed she'd never really left.

Martha didn't let on, but she resented a little her daughter's apparent reluctance to transplant herself to other soil. She'd been looking forward to the time alone with Roger, to their becoming reacquainted as husband and wife after twenty-two years as Nancy's mother and father. Not that she was sorry for those years—far from it—but hadn't they been happy together once, before Nancy?

If Roger felt any similar misgivings, he didn't show them. He hated change more than any man; felt, besides, the world was run by fools and charlatans. Probably it was part of his secret pride that his only child, his precious and talented daughter, who might have gone anywhere, done anything, had freely decided to stay with them.

It was the choices Nancy made after that, the ones involving her future husband, he couldn't abide. There was the scandal, of course: Warren Jimson was married, though separated from his wife. Particularly upsetting to Roger, Martha believed, was Warren's age—he was nearly as old as they were, with grown children of his own. Roger must have felt as if his daughter were replacing him. And so she was. "Warren's Daddy's age," Nancy allowed, "but he's still curious about the world."

It didn't help that Warren planned to move away with her. He was a veterinarian with a dwindling practice, and he wanted to go to Appalachia, eventually retire there, where his skills would do the most good. Nancy would be his assistant; Nancy, who'd never even owned a pet. Roger was against the marriage, against the move. "Don't delude yourself," he warned his daughter. "It's going to be a hard life."

"But it's going to be our life," she said. After that, Nancy never discussed with her father any of her plans regarding Warren.

Roger refused to attend the wedding. "You have to go," his wife told him, foreseeing the consequences if he didn't. Nancy, who was too much like him, would be slow to forgive such a slight. But accepting what he didn't like, even when it was inevitable, had never been a trait of his. Martha was furious with him. The day of the wedding, after she returned from the ceremony, she tracked him down in the garden, where he was pruning the Japanese ornamentals, and proceeded to describe every detail of the occasion—how Nancy looked, what she wore, everything. After all, their daughter's marriage, unwelcome though it might have been, was part of nature's bounty as much as his precious flowers, and it was wrong, it was downright sinful, of him to ignore it. She told him so. Roger let her talk, going about his business with the pruning shears. When at last she fell silent, he let the shears drop to his side. He stood there in his garden, staring at her. His eyes could not have been colder than if she'd been one of those witches come down from the mountain.

Oh, she knew exactly how hurt he was losing his daughter. Wasn't she hurt, too? She felt desolate when Nancy later sent the photograph showing where they were living—on the side of a mountain, in a trailer, their front yard dense with overgrowth. Martha couldn't imagine a place more different from the one where Nancy had grown up. In the photograph, there were two somber looking men in hats standing with the newlyweds by the front door; Nancy hadn't bothered to identify them. Studying the picture, peering at those unknown faces, Martha questioned the purpose of being a parent at all. Had they raised their daughter only so she could go to live among strangers, and worse, be a stranger herself?

Then she remembered the cold look her husband had given her in the garden, and that made her feel even more alone. Maybe Nancy wasn't the only stranger she'd been sharing her life with all these years.

ROGER TELLS HER the thunder from last night's storm sounded hollow and theatrical, like someone moving furniture around in the attic. "I can't believe it didn't wake you," he says.

"You should have called me." It makes her feel terrible, the thought of him lying there all by himself in the middle of the night.

She goes out right after breakfast to check on the garden and finds it littered with leaves and sticks, its soil rent by gullies. It looks as if it's been broken into and ransacked, but the thieves have overlooked the real treasure. Amid the wreckage, dozens of new blooms, as if startled prematurely from their beds by last night's thunder, have burst forth in brilliant reds, yellows, and purples.

Martha would like to pick some of the flowers, surprise him with them. He could see then how well she's done her job. The trouble is, he doesn't believe in picking flowers. It's one of his principles. And he's too weak to get to the window to look outside. She offered before to take photographs of the garden, but he said no, she should just describe her progress, he could picture it all in his head. Such an idealist he's turned into! If he didn't have to keep his wife occupied, he might dispense with seeds, dirt, and fertilizer altogether.

"Ssst, get out of here!" Martha says, spotting a cat creeping among the peonies. "Go on!" The animal pauses, sizing her up with its insolent stare. The cat is silvery gray, the color of ashes in a fireplace. Martha's never seen it before and figures it must be new around here. The neighborhood cats know to avoid this garden. Roger prizes bird song almost above flowers and has for years waged war on the local felines. Martha glances instinctively up at his window, as if he might be peeking from behind the drawn shade, waiting to see what she will do.

From the basket of implements she carries on her arm, she chooses the garden claw and sets the basket down. Then, claw in hand, she rushes the animal. It flees down the path that leads into Roger's boxwood maze—a mistake: the cat will be cornered when it comes to the dead end where the path runs into the greenhouse. Martha means to give it a good scare, is all, score a small victory for her husband in his long battle against invaders.

But the cat is nowhere in sight when she arrives puffing at the end of the twisting route. Instead Martha is confronted by evidence of her own treachery—five rows of vegetables she planted last week, which the storm has left miraculously unscathed. Roger favors beauty and whimsy in his garden; he abhors the merely practical. Martha, on the other hand, told herself as long as she was breaking her back she deserved to get something out of it. She'd enjoyed the feeling of defiance, pressing the seeds of beans and cucumbers into this pampered soil, staking the homely looking packet pictures over the furrows, imagining tomato and onion sandwiches in August. Now as she surveys this plot of earth, which will yield its harvest only after her husband is gone, she feels keenly her betrayal.

"Martha!" It's Roger calling, anxious no doubt to know the condition of his garden. She looks up from the work of her hands to where the greenhouse, shimmering in the early morning sun, throws back her reflection. Cloaked in an old, black duster, her eyes shaded from the light by a man's felt hat, she hardly cuts the figure of a dutiful servant. Why, anyone seeing her would think she was an intruder in this garden or, given the evidence of that lethal tool she's clutching, something worse.

WHEN FATHER NARO comes, he crosses to the window and raises the shade in Roger's room. "Let there be light," he says, chuckling at the conceit. He stands there, his back to them, looking down at the garden. What must he think of it, that fanciful nursery in which no statue of St. Francis presides and the teasing forms of nymphs and satyrs dwell among the foliage? The priest's idea of natural beauty is the golf course where he spends much of his free time. Golfing metaphors dot his sermons, and Roger used to say that Father Naro pictured heaven itself as a big clubhouse on a hill where the Son of Man reigned as local pro.

What would paradise be for her husband, Martha wonders. A garden, naturally—one infinitely various, cunningly devised, with endless paths to amble down. For a companion he would choose not an old woman but a little girl, one constant and true, in a plaid jumper.

As if the priest has read her mind, he says, "When I look at your garden, I remember Nancy at her first communion party, running in and out of the flowers with her plastic watering can."

"It was tin," Martha says. "It was green, with lilies painted on it." She found the can on a shelf in Roger's greenhouse the other day, next to a pair of little flannel gloves and a straw bonnet with paper flowers.

"Ah, well," Father Naro says, "she was so full of life and joy, she looked so brand new that day I thought, here's one of God's own angels."

What he doesn't know, what Martha has confided to no one, is that "God's own angel" has so far been noncommittal about visiting her dying father. Roger would never forgive Martha if he knew she had asked her. Like Nancy, he is unbending. They both have their principles. They can tell you what they are. Father and daughter remind Martha of the two goats in one of the fables they used to read. When the goats meet on a narrow mountain pass, neither will yield the way, so both end up tumbling over the side. The last few years Martha has felt powerless to prevent a similar tragedy in her family. All she can do is watch the two of them fall.

Yesterday she committed a sin. It was after she came across the watering can, the gloves, the flowered bonnet. They made her think what a wonderful father he'd been and how poorly fatherhood had repaid him. Standing there in the greenhouse, she said, "I will never forgive Nancy for not coming." She said each word deliberately, right to God. A sin in anyone's book.

Roger lies with his eyes closed, bathed in the light Naro has let in. He has not spoken of his daughter in almost three years, and Martha does not believe he will do so now. His eyes are closed not because the light hurts them but because he doesn't need eyes to see what his priest and his wife are up to here.

If you're so damned smart then, Martha thinks, why don't you tell us what it's like to die all alone?

As she arranged beforehand with Father Naro, she excuses herself. "I'll be in the garden." On her way downstairs she strains to hear their voices, but they don't even seem to be talking.

By a trick of light, House Mountain looks close enough today that you could hit it with a rock. They may be getting another storm. She'll need to cover the hibiscus seedlings or they'll be washed away this time for sure. With a glance back at the bedroom window, she heads for the greenhouse, where Roger keeps a roll of plastic sheeting. When she returns with the sheeting, there's singing coming from the bedroom.

Martha stops where she is. It's Roger's voice, sweet and clear in spite of its thinness. He's always had a lovely voice, though he pretends to think otherwise. When he sang the hymns in church, people would turn around to see where the sound was coming from.

It's not a hymn coming from his window now:

Ay, yi, yi, yi,
Gone now is sadness.
Your floating eyes
Are like a paradise.
They bring gladness,
De lo lindo.

Martha can't help feeling mocked by the words, standing beneath his window, like a spurned lover. The song is one Nancy used to sing in grade school, one they all remember. His singing it now helps confirm what she has suspected all along: despite his long silence on the subject of his daughter, Roger has never let go of her. Nancy's the one he pines for, has never stopped pining for. In her absence, not even death matters to him—or it matters so much, coming as the final proof of his loss, it can't be faced at all.

"Don't ask me," Father Naro says, when they meet a few minutes later in the garden. "I suggested we pray together. He said, 'Let's sing instead.'"

"What happened after that?"

"Nothing. He's asleep. He went to sleep on me." The priest's eyes won't meet hers.

"He's playing possum," Martha says, setting her jaw and staring up at the window.

"I heard him snoring, Martha!"

She resists the urge to grab him by the shoulders, turn him around, and push him back in the house. "Get in there and do your job!" she'd like to tell the priest. "I'm doing mine!"

"Maybe sleep is a blessing for him," Father Naro says.

Martha shakes her head. Sleep is just one more barrier to keep her out.

"I could come again tomorrow," he offers.

"Never mind."

His hurt expression causes her instant regret. "It's not your fault," she says. What on earth did she expect him to accomplish anyway? For penance she offers up her gnarled hand to him at the garden gate, lets him press it in his two-fisted golfer's grip until the tears come into her eyes. Then she carries the hand with her upstairs to check on her sleeping husband.

She bends over him, puts her ear close to his lips, as if waiting to hear a secret. The feel of his breath on her cheek momentarily reassures her.

His hands are folded on his chest—the right posture for death. Yet the long, shapely hands frighten and exasperate her by how unprepared they are. Sticking out of the pajama sleeves, they look as naked and innocent as a boy's, giving the lie to how hard they've worked, all they've touched and held. He never cared for jewelry, wears to this day no wedding band, only the college ring he's had ever since she knew him. The light reflecting off the stone in the ring makes a crystalline green star on the bedroom ceiling, and Martha feels a catlike impulse to snatch at it.

LOOSE CHANGE

He grabs me from behind and jams a bony knee up my skirt between my "buns of steel," which, believe me, are tighter than anything you've seen on those cheesy exercise commercials. The chain he presses against my throat gives me hope. It's a delicate thing, wispy as a skank's ankle bracelet. You couldn't strangle one of my gerbils with it. (Their little claws are going lickety-split over in the cage.) I'm like, "You're scaring the rodents."

He drives his knee upward, nearly lifting me off my toes. "Mi padre, bless me, a sinner." His dry lips flutter against my ear. "Say it!"

So I say it. Adding, just to move things along, "It's been three years since my last confession."

"Liar!" he says. "You went just last week."

"Anyway, it feels like three years."

He tells me all I've done—disgusting things, half of them not even true. "You've been talking to that Amber Rutland," I say. A notorious skank.

"I been talking to no one, I talk to you."

"Fine, then!" I'm getting ticked. "Would you kindly remove your knee from under my skirt?" It's embarrassing but sometimes I open my mouth and it's my mother's voice that comes out. He does what I say though. I open my mouth again and this time it's my father's voice, plain as can be: "Who do you think you are, barging in here? How'd you get past the electronic shield, the guards?"

He laughs. I've finally said something he expected. He slides the chain off my throat, whispers something—I only catch the words "human sacrifice"—then lets go of me with a push. Not a hard push though. Despite the bony knee and harsh words, I feel a hidden tenderness in the way he handles me, as if he believed I was truly fragile.

Before I can turn around, there's a sound like beating wings, a rush of air. I look and he's gone.

The pitter-patter of little feet has stopped in the gerbils' cage. There's no sound at all to disturb the quiet of the larger cage I call home—just somewhere, far off, the muffled churning of an ice maker, as if the big old house were politely clearing its throat.

THE NEXT NIGHT my angel comes again but I still haven't seen his face. He wears a leopard-skin cowl with a crown of feathers—each one plucked from a bird of prey, he says. I'm curious about the costume, and he seems willing to entertain questions until I ask where he hides the wings. Then his full lips, which are cracked and flecked with blood, curl into a profound scowl. I drop my eyes, turn pigeon toes in my ballet slippers. I'm wearing an off-the-shoulder pink leotard, my hair pulled back—no make-up, no jewelry. I'm all clean lines. Just for him.

He stands with his feet spread, his arms folded on his naked and hairless chest. "I am Joselito." He announces it like a challenge, as if the name's caused him trouble in the past. Hearing him say it, I picture the fat Mexican mama whose favorite he probably was and the older brothers and sisters who always made fun of him. I want to tell him everything will be all right, he doesn't have to act tough with me.

Joselito says I have plenty to answer for. He says I first came to his attention at the Columbia Mall. He was behind me in a long line at the Dairy Heaven. He says when it was my turn I ordered a Happy Isles Sundae and dumped two fistfuls of change on the counter. The coins went everywhere. Customers had to wait while people in paper hats and aprons dropped to their knees all over the store. Joselito says when at last my change was counted out and my sundae delivered into my hands, I walked out with my ice cream, tossing the leftover coins in the trash container by the door.

He gets pretty upset telling about this. There are tears of rage in his eyes. I suppose it wouldn't do any good to set him straight, tell him it was my friend Marcie who pulled that stunt in the ice cream store. (Ten minutes later she's in the public toilet with a finger down her throat.) When you look like me, you're the one they remember, you're the one they blame. Like the other day, my social studies teacher is on us about the extermination of the Indians in Nicaragua. (Nee-ca-rah-gwa, he says, rolling the "r." A real *paisano*.) And I swear he's glaring at me the whole time. I finally go, "Excuse me, I don't even know where the Mosquito Coast is."

"I know you don't," he says, in this voice that's sad and snotty at the same time. "I know you don't."

Joselito's a lot cuter than my social studies teacher but with both of them you get the impression no matter what you do you're the one who's always wrong.

MY PETS START turning up dead. First the gerbils die in their sleep, curled against each other in a little pile. The gardener discovers my collie dog lifeless among the begonias. One of the kittens lies in a ball on my father's putting green, a light breeze ruffling its white fur.

It's a bloodless and oddly beautiful massacre. Still I shudder to think when and where the others may be discovered. My father orders autopsies on the animals and the security force increased. At dinner he speaks in veiled terms of "those who would wish us harm." I sit staring moist-eyed at my reflection inside the flowered ring on my plate. My shoulders start to quiver and I can't stop them. "John!" my mother says, meaning my father should leave off his paranoid rantings and comfort his little girl. If I'd loved the pets better, I sob, if I'd taken better care of them, they wouldn't have died. My daddy takes me on his lap and all through dessert tries soothing me with promises of Senegal parrots, mandrills from western Africa, lemurs from Madagascar. I picture the faces of all the animals he might buy, like masks ranged against us, and from behind each one the fierce and loving gaze of my angel, Joselito, tears my flesh to shreds.

IT WAS A necessary thing, the death of the animals, Joselito says. He's strutting back and forth in front of the aquarium, where nothing survived his purge except a hermit crab. I don't think he knows about the crab or he'd mention the reason it was spared. So here's an endearing chink in my angel's armor.

"I must make room for myself in your life," he's saying.

"I want that, too."

He doesn't believe me. "Your parents are next."

He's bluffing. My parents are beyond his reach. I'm beyond his reach for that matter. He comes because I invite him. I dress for him specially every night after dinner, and I wait, rehearsing a nameless guilt that makes him possible.

Joselito says the first time he saw me I was in front of him in the line for confessions at Holy Redeemer Church.

It might be true. I sometimes steal a visit with the priest there, who, unlike Joselito, keeps a sense of humor about his job. Father Hicks is black; over the tarnished brass grate that separates him from me in that little compartment of hell, he's posted a handmade sign—a black-faced stick figure wearing a big grin above his Roman collar, with the caption "A Shine to Make Your Soul Shine!" I think it's important for an authority figure to be able to laugh at himself. I know I plan to.

Joselito says I have no shame. Haven't I ever heard of whispering my sins? The people in line could hear every word of my confession. They all scattered among the pews, trying to get out of earshot. When I came out of the confessional, he says, my face was as bland as a plaster saint's. I acted like I was the Queen of Peace and had just crushed the Serpent beneath my sandaled foot. According to him, I did not kneel to say my penance but made straight for the door, where I dropped several coins in the poor box on my way out. Joselito says he felt the hollow clatter of those coins in his own breast.

WHAT'S WRONG, I wonder. Since his first visit, my angel hasn't touched me. "Your poor hands," I say. His nails are jagged and cracked, some split down to the quick. His knuckles are mostly skinned or caked with dirt. He pulls his hands away, glowering. I place the silky palm of my own hand on his chest and force myself to meet his stare. I'm wearing a green satin nightshirt that slides across my skin with every movement. It makes me deliciously aware of myself, makes me feel, more than all my father's guards and alarms, precious. "I won't break," I assure my angel, praying it isn't true.

Joselito says the time has come for him to meet my parents. I drop my hand from his chest. "My parents? I've been expecting them to turn up dead. Now you want me to introduce you?"

"You are embarrassed of me?"

For an angel of the Lord, he's pretty dense. "If you must know," I tell him, "I don't want to share you with anyone." It's the truth, and Joselito is pleased to hear it. His chest puffs; the pure white crests of his wings wink at me over his skinny shoulders. I hope this moment will be a new beginning for us, but the shit-eating grin my angel trains on me isn't a good sign. My friend Marcie is probably right, it's always a mistake to let them know you care.

JOSELITO SHEDS THE cowl and feathers to meet my parents. For them he wears gray slacks and a shirt decorated with parrots. His thick, black hair is neatly parted and combed. His ravaged hands he keeps hidden in his pockets. Not that anyone would notice his hands, his face is so beautiful. My mother, whose own face hangs in the waiting rooms of cosmetic surgeons from here to Palm Beach, can't stop looking at him. She tells my angel he has the eyes of Bianca Jagger and the bone structure of "that Somalian model, the one who married David Bowie."

"She means that as a compliment," my father says, clapping a hand on his blushing young visitor's shoulder. I have an anxious moment as Joselito staggers under the weight of that hand. Now that he's insisted on meeting my parents, I do hope he'll make a good impression. When my mother asks me to check on the refreshments, Joselito gives me an anxious look. I blow my angel a kiss behind their backs. "I won't be long."

As it turns out, I didn't have to worry. When I return the three of them are sitting together on the couch, tongues of fire licking up from the grate in front of them, everything as cozy as if they were posing for the family Christmas card. Joselito's telling my parents about the first time he saw them. He says my mother and father had driven into the city to attend a concert. The neighborhood was a dangerous one, so when my father spied some ragged boys standing in the limbs of a tree near the back of a vacant lot, he waved them over. He gave them each a quarter and told them if they watched his car there would be more money when he returned. "I was one of those boys," Joselito says.

"Daddy, you never go anywhere without a security team," I remind him. But he doesn't even hear me. Joselito's talking.

Joselito says the other boys decided to take their quarters and go. "To hell with this rich man's car," one of them said, giving a karate kick to the fender. When Joselito insisted on staying to do the job he was paid for, the others beat him up and took his money.

"C'mon, did that really happen?" I say. The fire in the grate crackles, a log shifts and falls heavily, sending up sparks.

Joselito reaches inside his shirt and pulls out a thin chain, which must be the same one he held against my throat that first night. Hanging from the chain is a silver coin. "This is the fifty-cent piece," Joselito says, "that your father gave to me when he returned."

My mother leans close to him, taking the coin gently in her burnished fingertips. She rubs her thumb several times over the profile of the handsome, martyred president of her youth, as if to clean away the tarnish from what she's always claimed was an idealistic childhood. "Only fifty cents," she says, looking at my father. "For such loyalty, such suffering. Shame! Shame on us!"

JOSELITO LIKES MY parents better than me. Why am I not surprised? It's that way with every living thing I bring home. That's why I was secretly glad when he murdered the pets. They were mine in name only. Their dumb eyes brightened only when my mother or father came near, as if the animals knew instinctively who it was made their world turn.

Joselito no longer visits me in my room. He and my parents sit for hours in front of the fire downstairs, while I hide on the landing, listening to my angel's voice. I can't make out what he's telling them, but one thing I know, it's not flattering to me. My parents have grown "concerned" about me. They told me so the other night at dinner. They said I shouldn't treat their concern as a burden but as an expression of their love. They speak as if they were bestowing a gift, one of those special adult gifts I'm not wise enough yet to appreciate but will someday learn to cherish.

They're concerned, for one thing, that I've stopped eating. The "A" word hangs in the air but they're too polite to use it. If they only knew about my other mortifications of the flesh, their concern might grow into fear. *The Lives of the Saints* has become my guide. I've devised a harness of underthings that makes my slightest movement uncomfortable and even painful. My sunken eyes, my hollow cheeks, these cause distress on the faces of my parents and even friends. But to me they are signs an invisible world exists, that it has consequences, and that I have been permitted to enter it.

Another thing. Either I'm pregnant, which is impossible, or I've simply stopped having my period. Praise God.

JOSELITO DECIDES TO lower himself by visiting me in my room. He wears the cowl and feathers like old times. He says my sacrifices are not redemptive because they are driven by pride. Besides that, my parents are worried sick.

"I miss our times together," I tell him. But who am I kidding? Things have changed between us. Maybe it's for the best. My parents talk of adopting him, and while Joselito pretends indifference to this scheme, I think he likes the idea of becoming the son they never had. My brother.

I am a spoiled baby, Joselito says. My parents deserve better from me. I roll my eyes. He partially unfurls his wings, trying to intimidate me. Like brother and sister, we're already learning to get on each other's nerves.

When he's gone, I go to the aquarium and tap on the glass, summoning the hermit crab Joselito wasn't powerful enough to kill. I unwrap the wadded-up paper towel in which I keep his raw hamburger. The look and smell of the meat turns my stomach, but once I drop it in the water it's fun to see my pet nab it in his claws and scuttle into his shell with the prize. It gives me pleasure, too, watching the flecks of leftover meat, blood, and gristle float to the surface, knowing the crab is inside his shell steadily chewing, getting stronger.

AT SCHOOL JOSELITO is welcomed as a foreign exchange student and invited to speak at assembly. He talks to us in moving terms about his family back home and the hardships they have to endure. There's also something puzzling at the end of his speech about the need for human sacrifice as a remedy for suffering.

In the aftermath of my angel's appearance, hysterical remorse grips the school. Extra help has to be called in to handle the overflow in the counseling office. The headmaster gets on the intercom to say Joselito has assured him the mention of human sacrifice was only a figure of speech. Nevertheless, several girls pass me notes for Joselito, each one signed "Love" and each volunteering to be his victim, or as Amber Rutland puts it, his "lamb without blemish," which must be an example of what my English teacher means by poetic license.

Some of the instructors are acting strange, too. I find myself cornered in the lunch room by my social studies teacher, who says he's worried about me. Do I feel all right? He feasts his gaze on my bony frame, stares deep into my eyes, where, if he squints, he might just glimpse a shadow of the third world he's so in love with. Before he leaves he fills out a piece of paper and makes me promise to see a counselor right away. The truth is, I wouldn't mind talking to someone, but the counselors are so over-scheduled the only thing they can offer me is a boiler room chat with the custodian the first of next week. So I pay a visit to Father Hicks.

At my knock the man of God slides open his little window. I bow my head, trying to think where to begin. "Bless me, Father, for I have sinned," he prompts, as if I were new at this.

"C'mon, you know me."

He peers through the latticed grate, face like a scorched waffle. "The Angel of Death?"

"Very funny."

"What happened?" he says. "You used to be such a healthy young sinner."

I pour out the story of my suffering, all about Joselito, how he murdered my pets, broke my heart, then stole the affections of my parents and friends.

"You must love him very much," the priest says.

"I'm learning to get over it."

THE FEATHERS HE'S begun to shed all over the house convince me he has no plans to leave us soon. At dinner I pick a downy, white plume out of my water glass and hold it up, dripping, for all to see. "This is what it must be like to live on a chicken ranch," I say, but nobody laughs. Joselito's face is as red as the meat on his plate.

Last night I caught him sneaking down the hallway with a pillowcase, picking up stray feathers. It made me think how respectable he's become since he first introduced himself by shoving a knee up my ass. His new clothes and manicured nails don't fool me. I know him better than my parents. Right now he'd like to grab the meat off his plate and rip it with his teeth. He'd like to do the same to me. Though with me all he'd get is a mouthful of bones and bile.

"Marcie thinks Joselito's cute," I announce to the table, watching my adopted brother's face turn an even deeper red.

"Your friend's probably a little young for Joselito," says my mother, who'd like to keep him for herself.

"Marcie's mature for her age," I say.

"That's the truth," my father says, winking at Joselito.

An intention begins to form itself. "It would mean a lot to her, Joselito," I say, "if we planned it so you just ran into her at the mall sometime. No big date or anything." I stretch a skinny arm out on the table, toward my angel. I do a little tap dance with my fingers on the mahogany, the blue veins in my arm twisting like snakes. "Please! For me."

What can he say? It's understood around here that, in my present condition, even my whims need to be honored.

"It's set, then," I say. "I'll be the chaperone."

COLUMBIA MALL IS celebrating the season. Under the vaulted glass ceiling of the rotunda, the Easter Bunny sits inside a giant egg. With his slanted glass eyes and huge buckteeth, he looks like the picture of the Imperial Ruler in my history book. The whole place is filled with the sound of wailing children, those begging to get in line, those already in line but afraid to sit on the bunny's lap the closer they get to those menacing teeth. The way my head's starting to pound, I feel like wailing myself.

Marcie wants a picture with the Easter Bunny. "C'mon, I'll sit on one knee and you can sit on the other," she says to Joselito.

My angel won't go for it. Never mind he used to prowl around in mask and feathers. "He thinks this is beneath his dignity," I explain to Marcie.

"He's with the wrong girls, then," she says.

Joselito's figured that much out. He keeps looking up at the glass dome, as if it might offer a means of escape. I put my arm across his back, fondling with my fingertips the sharp points of his shoulder blades. "I wouldn't try it," I say, "not with the condition your poor wings are in." He shrugs my arm away, casting a sheepish glance at Marcie.

Marcie still wants a picture but she's willing to pass on the bunny. "I've got a better idea," she says. She takes Joselito by one arm, I take the other, and together we guide him along the promenade. "Relax," I say, nudging him playfully. My angel wears the intense but unfocused expression of a blind man, as if he were concentrating on something in front of him that his eyes can't make out. My headache is gone. In its place is a feeling like rushing wind and bright light. As we approach the down-escalator, picking our way among the false vegetation, I feel somehow as if we were coming to the lip of a canyon.

"I remember the first time I saw you," I tell Joselito in a half-sung sigh. "It was down there by the fountain. I was six, you couldn't have been much older. You were leaning over the edge of the fountain with your sleeve pushed up, picking coins out of the water. I complained to my father: 'That boy is stealing people's wishes!' He gave me a penny and said, 'You have to throw it far out, in the middle, where he can't get it.' So I did. That's when I made the wish of all wishes, the one none of the characters in the fairy stories ever think to make. You know the one. I wished that all my wishes would come true."

Marcie says, "That's pretty smart for six years old."

"I thought it was working, too. My father let me eat all the ice cream and candy I wanted. Later my stomach swelled up and I was sick all night. Mother was furious with Daddy, but I knew it wasn't his fault. It was the secret wish I'd made, growing inside me, poisoning me with its slyness and greed."

"Kids!" Marcie says. "What imaginations!"

I feel a shiver pass through Joselito. "Don't be afraid, my pet," I say, not unkindly.

"Here it is," Marcie says. We turn in under the fake movie marquee with the lights blinking and my name up in big block letters, like I was the only one they were expecting. The place is called Cinematique, and Marcie orders the Exotic Locations Special for all of us. They do our hair and faces. They dress

Marcie and me in identical white robes with gold lamé belts. "You're the virgins," the wardrobe guy informs us with a smirk.

Joselito's the star—the high priest. When he walks in and stands in front of the backdrop with the volcano on it, I'm almost sorry we missed our chance to be more than brother and sister. My angel is as fierce and beautiful as an Aztec god. "Only, lose the necklace," I tell him. It's the same cheap one he's always worn. "It doesn't go with the rest."

Marcie agrees. "It spoils the effect."

Is it so much to ask? But Joselito is stubborn as usual. He stands there as if he thought he was carved out of stone. All the times I threw myself at him come back to me. I did everything but kiss his feet. I go, "Once a beaner always a beaner." He claps his hand over the fifty-cent piece he claims my father gave him, as if daring me to do something about it. A hot bubble that has been rising in my chest suddenly bursts in my throat, and a sound escapes me that will be humiliating to recall later—like the snarl of a cornered animal, though it's Joselito about to go on the defensive. I fly at him and we both crash through the volcano. We go plummeting. It's a free fall—bottomless. No need to worry the air with wings. There's screaming in my ears, and it must be mine, but I'm not a bit afraid.

The next thing I know Marcie is trying to pull me off him. "Let go," she says. "Let go of him—now!" When she finally manages to pry my hands open, the coin and its delicate links of chain slip through my fingers and disappear like quick silver. I gaze down at my angel. His eyes are fixed in a stare that won't look at me. It's his final snub.

I FIGURE I'VE got some explaining to do at home. I didn't mean to kill him, I'll say. Who would have thought the chain was so strong and his neck so weak?

"Sorry we're late," Marcie says to my parents. "We've been at the Food Court. You should have seen her eat."

"That's wonderful news," my mother says, hugging me tight. I let out a burp—a belch, actually, one so big and violent it's like an exorcism. My mother holds me at arm's length, a look of transport on her face. You'd think I'd just spoken in tongues. "John," she says to my father, "our daughter is back."

I'm like, "About your son—"

"The thing about him was," my mother says with a far-off look, "he never knew the meaning of the word knock."

"Not only that," my father says. "Rolf told me no way he gets a sanitized clearance."

"He *was* an angel," I remind them, though why I should be the one sticking up for Joselito is a mystery to me. Especially since I'm not sure we've seen the last of him. It would be just like him to pull some stunt—show up at dinner uninvited; sit in my chair and glare at me like Banquo's ghost.

But at dinner I feel only the approving gaze of my parents upon my bowed head as I polish off every pea and carrot on the plate, then pat my lips clean with a snow-white napkin—a good girl at last.

Still, I tell myself, he might be waiting in ambush upstairs. I slip into my room, determined not to be taken by surprise. "Joselito, I know you're here." But the flicker of movement I detect in the corner of my eye turns out to be nothing more than the hermit crab darting into its shell.

There's always sleep, I think. Joselito may haunt my dreams.

I tap on the glass of the aquarium. "I'm lonely," I complain to my pet. But the crab only stares at me from inside its shell, with beady, frightened eyes, and will not come out to play.

THE WEDNESDAY
LADY

D ee Plogger had her key in the lock and her hand firmly on the doorknob when she felt the brass twist in her
palm. Then the door jerked open, pulling her across
the threshold.

"Miss Plogger, hello! Didn't mean to startle you." He was
wearing a purple terry-cloth robe that exposed the tufted gray hair
on his chest. His skinny legs and knobby ankles were also on dis-
play, if anyone cared to look. "We just got in last night," he said.

"I figured you'd be along sooner or later. No one said when."
She'd been arriving here every Wednesday to an empty house for
nearly three months. She preferred it that way. Now that Mrs.
Chalmers, his former wife, had gone to live with her sister in
Florida, let it stay empty. Dee Plogger meant to keep the house
as she always had, the way Mrs. Chalmers liked it.

"You've been very patient with us," David Chalmers said,
"through all the—uncertainty." He slipped around behind her
and wrestled the gray trench coat from her broad shoulders,
dropping it across a chair near the door. Dee made a mental note
to return later and hang the coat where it belonged. "There's
someone I want you to meet," he said.

She followed him down the hall past the luggage stacked at the bottom of the stairs. A pair of skis, with a floppy straw hat perched on top, jutted up from the middle of the pile. David Chalmers went almost at a trot, past the music and sewing rooms, back toward the kitchen. "Macy!" he called. "Macy, dear!" Dee let him go, determined to arrive in her own time. She did not take lightly her responsibility in meeting the new wife. She thought of the ladies whose houses she'd been cleaning for years; until now always the same five women—one for each day of the week, Monday through Friday. Her ladies, Dee called them; fine women who lived in fine homes; all dear friends of the first Mrs. Chalmers. They were like unseen witnesses to what would follow.

The new Mrs. Chalmers was sitting at the breakfast table, a triangle of toast poised before her very red lips, *The Weekly Gazette* spread out flat in front of her. She had one leg folded under her, and the first thing Dee thought was, she's got her foot on the embroidered seat cushion. The second thing she thought was, how unnatural men are. She'd known the new wife would be young; news of that had preceded the Chalmers to town. But this girl was young enough to be one of David Chalmers' daughters. Why, she was almost young enough to be Dee's daughter, who, if she'd lived, would have been twenty-two.

The poor thing, thought Dee, who could not have said whether she meant her daughter or the young woman in front of her. Though her Penny had died shortly after birth, Dee didn't think of her as frozen in infancy forever; she pictured her on some parallel and invisible plane, growing apace with other children, going through what they went through—school, braces, dates. But marriage! Dee hadn't gotten around to imagining her Penny with a man. Certainly not a man David Chalmers' age. Behind them in the hall, the old clock that had stood mute for three months slowly ground its gears, then erupted in a spasm of striking.

"Miss Plogger is a local treasure," Chalmers was saying. "If it weren't for her this old mausoleum, for one, would go to rack and ruin."

"It's easy to see that somebody who loves the place has been looking after it," the girl said, coming forward to shake Dee's hand. In the housekeeper's experience, only women in suits, on TV, shook hands. This one wasn't wearing any suit. She had on jeans and a t-shirt and, except for her red lipstick, little makeup. She had one of those modern haircuts, skinned around the neck, with a heavy swatch falling over one eye. The concealed eye made her look shy or sneaky, Dee couldn't decide which.

"I don't know a soul here," the girl said. She let go of Dee's hand. "You're the first one I've met."

"The first of many," her husband said. "People are friendly here, aren't they, Miss Plogger?"

"Can be," Dee said. "About that luggage in the front hall, you want me to take it upstairs?"

"No, no, I'll tote the luggage," David Chalmers said. "You two stay and get acquainted."

He left them, and Dee began clearing the breakfast dishes. The girl returned to her *Weekly Gazette*. "Plogger,'" she said. "There's a picture of a Plogger here in the paper." She held it up. A man in a baseball cap cradled a squash as big and round as a woman's behind; the man looked very pleased with himself. Dee had seen the picture already. It was her cousin Jimmie Plogger, and she thought once again that, of the two in the photograph, the squash had more brains.

"He never even grew it," Dee said, using her fingers to rub lipstick off the rim of the cup she was holding under the faucet. "His mother, my aunt, grew that squash."

"Really?"

"Everybody knows it."

"Are there hard feelings?"

"Not about that."

"Oh." Macy Chalmers pulled the hank of hair to one side of her face like it was a curtain and stared at Dee with two eyes. The girl had a sweet enough face, when you could see it. But she was nothing fancy, that was for sure. Dee supposed she'd been expecting something in stretch pants and stirrups, with glossy fingertips and a helmet of blonde hair. At first glance, this girl had none of the armor usually associated with grasping second wives. Too bad, Dee thought. She'll need armor.

The girl said she'd never run across the name Plogger before.

"It's a name hereabouts," Dee said. "You can't throw a rock in any direction and not hit a Plogger. You can't pick up a rock, not have a Plogger crawl out. Some say Plogger's what they call no-count in these parts."

"What?"

"No-count. White trash. Don't tell me you never heard of white trash."

"Yes," the girl said reluctantly. "But you're not saying—that—about yourself?"

Now it was Dee's turn to stare. "Heavens, no! Where are you from?"

DEE WONDERED WHAT her boyfriend, Jot, would think of Macy Chalmers. It never ceased to amaze her what men found appealing. For over twenty years, Jot Dooley had been her test-case male, but while he wasn't shy about expressing his opinions, she rarely felt the wiser for them.

"When I was finished for the day," she told him, "I had to hunt all over the house for her just so I could get paid." Jot was watching that scrawny blonde turn the letters on TV. Dee had read somewhere she couldn't even spell. "Where do you think I found her? In the attic, pawing through the family things."

"Her things now, I guess." He shifted the lever on the side of his chair and it bumped him forward in two jerky motions. "Buy a vowel, dummy," he urged one of the contestants.

"Said she was looking for pictures of David when he was a boy. Makes you wonder, doesn't it? If she's so interested in him when he was a boy, why'd she marry him when he's an old man?"

"That's easy," Jot said. "Women're attracted by older men."

"Ha, older men with money maybe! You think Macy Chalmers would give you the time of day?"

He pretended to study the word puzzle on the TV screen. "Something something RULE," he said.

You couldn't insult him. He let insults pass right by. "Anyway, that's not what I started to tell you," Dee said. "You got me off the subject. I finally found her up in the attic, told her I'm done for the day. Had my coat on and everything. So what's she do but keep me waiting while she looks for the checkbook. Then it's 'How much do I make this out for?' And 'Is that the amount you and David agreed on?' I told her, 'David's got nothing to do with it. All my business was with the lady of the house.'"

"What did she say to that?"

"Nothing. She shut up and wrote the check. If I hadn't given my promise to Mrs. Chalmers, I'd have quit on the spot."

"Give 'em hell, Dee."

She knew her indignation amused him. He had no capacity for outrage himself and therefore, she'd decided long ago, no self-respect. He lived hand-to-mouth, like an orphan child, in a run-down cabin in the woods, which he paid the rent on by working part-time as a house painter. Because the cabin had no phone, he took his business calls—what few there were—at Dee's place in the evenings. She'd overhear him with potential customers. "I'll slip over and have a look at that," he'd promise them. Or, "I'll slide by there sometime tonight, let you know what I think." Then he'd hang up the phone and go right back to the TV and his chair with the lever. It was his nature to be elusive where work was concerned. And other things, too. He had no family and few friends. Except for Dee and that easy chair, there was little to hold him in the world at all. She worried about him sometimes. It wasn't hard to imagine Jot slipping and sliding clean out of life itself.

"I got the funniest feeling," she said, "walking into that kitchen this morning, seeing that girl. She was so young, you know, it made me think of Penny for a second."

He looked at her with the wounded expression he wore whenever she brought up their dead daughter. "Don't, please, don't," the expression said. In an odd way she found it reassuring. If he was capable of being hurt, it meant he was still there.

"I can't help it," Dee said. "And that old man prancing around in his bathrobe! He's got daughters her age! You'd think that would stop him. You'd think being in the house where he lived with his wife for thirty years would stop him, or at least make him ashamed of himself."

"You said yourself, Dee, the Chalmers was separated. It's not like the girl stole him away."

"Men aren't ashamed, I know. What can you expect? It's the girl I blame more. Girls should know better, even young ones. There's one person disappointed in all this, I'll bet. That girl's mother. Wherever she is, she's ashamed."

Bells were ringing and lights were flashing up on the TV. The blonde extended her skinny little arms toward the completed puzzle, as if the words displayed on the screen were something clever she thought up herself. "The Golden Rule," Jot read.

"I remember this one," Dee said. "It's a repeat."

DEE HAD A postcard from the former Mrs. Chalmers in Florida. It showed a white bird on stick legs wading in a sunlit expanse of sand and water; among the shimmering blues and whites of the picture, the bird's shadow, stretching across the ground like a spear, seemed the most tangible thing. Dee, who could not imagine Evelyn Chalmers apart from her house, didn't like thinking of her in such surroundings. "Oh, Dee," the card said, "do you know what day it is? Wednesday. Our day together. How I miss your company and good common sense at times like these."

It was rumored that Evelyn Chalmers was suffering from ill health. Also, she and her sister weren't supposed to be getting along. The conventional wisdom among her friends—Dee's ladies—was that she should never have left town. "It's what I said all along," Dee told them.

But as a matter of fact, she understood perfectly the decision to move away. They all did. How could she be expected to stay and watch while another woman moved into her house, her life? It *was* hers. Never mind that David had inherited the place from his grandmother with the stipulation it stay in the family. In this house-proud little town, Evelyn Chalmers had carved a niche for herself, transforming the Victorian "cottage" on Thorn Hill Street into nothing less than a show place. How unfair that her husband should deprive her of it.

Men knew nothing of what it took to make a home, though they liked having one well enough. They were squatters by nature. Look at Jot and his cabin; the place was such a hovel Dee hadn't set foot in it for years. Even he knew something was missing there. Why else did he spend nearly every evening at her house? It was more than her telephone, her TV, her easy chair; it was more, too, than the meals she fed him, though if another man asked that's probably the reason he'd have given. That or sex, which would have been a lie; she and Jot rarely shared a bed anymore. Surely some part of him knew the truth; knew that someone who cared for him had made a place where he was welcome, where he could come anytime. But the significance of such a thing, if he understood it, no doubt slipped his mind.

Men forgot things. Look at David Chalmers. Some young girl with red lips peeks at him through her veil of hair and thirty years fly right out of his head. Still there was everything in that house to remind him of his former marriage. Mrs. Chalmers had taken very little with her. Her sister in Florida didn't have a lot of room, she said. Besides, she couldn't bear to see the old place gutted. "Gutted," that was her word. She'd rather leave it as it was, as she had created it over the years. Let the new woman work her changes. No doubt she would. In the meantime, it would make her feel better if Dee were around to keep an eye on things. "I don't want to know what happens," she said. "But you watch, Dee. You be my witness. It'll all be different inside a year. Just don't tell me. Bitterness is a terrible temptation."

So Dee watched, but little changed in the house. She did notice one Wednesday that someone had refolded all the bath and hand towels in the linen closet upstairs. It made her angry. She removed the towels, shook them out, folded them the proper way, and put them back again. This was war. But the following week the linen closet was just as she'd left it and that was the end of that.

As for Macy Chalmers, she made herself scarce when Dee was around. That was fine with Dee. She didn't need people underfoot when she was working. Not that there was much work to do on Wednesdays. Dee had to invent things, like polishing the brass doorknobs and hinges or replacing the shelving paper in the cabinets, because most of the cleaning, dusting, straightening, and laundering was already done when she arrived. At first she thought this was the girl's way of hinting she wasn't needed, but several weeks passed and nothing was mentioned about letting her go, so Dee wasn't sure what to make of it.

"Maybe she's just real neat," Jot said. "What do you care? Makes your job easier. You're getting paid, aren't you?"

Oh, yes, she was getting paid, and without any further trouble about the check. Always now, at the end of the day, the check was there, propped against Dee's purse on the table in the entrance hall, a "Thank You!" penned on the memo line in Macy Chalmers' looping, childlike hand. Some days the writing on that check was the only visible trace of the new Mrs. Chalmers to be found in the house. Dee should have been content; another battle won. She wasn't though. Like the house that never needed cleaning, the weekly check, waiting for her by the door every Wednesday, with its cheerful note scrawled across the bottom, was like an airy dismissal, was like a door slammed in her face.

"Standoffish," Dee said, when her ladies asked what the new woman was like. And yet Macy Chalmers hadn't seemed that way at first. Dee told Jot, "It's like she's, I don't know—hiding."

He laughed. "From you, you mean. Dee, maybe you shouldn't have been so hard on her."

"Somebody needs to be."

DEE WAS NO snoop. Ask any of the ladies she worked for and they would tell you: never was a door closed or a cabinet locked against Dee Plogger. So she blamed the girl's evasiveness for what happened next. She blamed the extra time she had on her hands every Wednesday. These were the factors that provoked her, though she reminded herself there was a principle involved as well. Didn't she owe it to Mrs. Chalmers to find out what sort of woman had moved into her home?

She began by peeking into dresser drawers in the master bedroom, without, however, venturing to disturb any of the neatly stacked contents. Eventually she dug deeper, pulling out some of the drawers and sifting through them. She was a little surprised at what nice things the girl owned, and what womanly things—silk scarves, embroidered handkerchiefs, fine jewelry, and the like. All Dee ever saw her in were jeans and a t-shirt; it was as if Macy Chalmers, though a married woman and mistress of a large house, still thought of herself as a teenager. Even so, Dee found few mementoes of girlhood in the bedroom dresser. One exception was a blue, leatherette diary secreted among some underwear. (It was fancy underwear, black and fretted with lace; a present from old David Chalmers, she would have bet money.) On the cover of the diary a barefoot child with her hair falling down pulled a wagon along a dusky path flanked on either side by sunflowers. The tall flowers' heads drooped over the child like a bunch of old maids; tut, tut, tut, they seemed to say. Though the diary's strap lock was broken and no impediment, Dee resisted temptation and left the book undisturbed in its nest of lingerie. She congratulated herself on showing such restraint; it almost seemed to justify her other invasions.

Once, in the bedroom closet, she found what must have been the girl's wedding dress. She lifted its plastic cover and ran her finger and thumb along the satin hem. Then she grew bolder, removing the cover completely and spreading the dress full-length on the bed. The gown was lovely, with lace sleeves and a beaded silk bodice. The color was not what Dee would have chosen for a daughter of hers; it was gray, almost the shade of tarnished silver. No girl's marriage, she felt, should begin as a compromise. Still it was a beautiful dress, and Dee stood there in the undisturbed silence of the big house, picturing what Macy Chalmers must have looked like in it.

"Funny thing is," she told Jot, "there isn't a picture of that girl's family anywhere in the place."

He had no idea just how extensively she'd searched. "Maybe she don't have family," he said.

She looked at him, surprised; it was something to consider. As the oldest of eight children, Dee tended to think of family as a fact of life. Not that having relatives necessarily made you less lonely, but it did make the world seem "furnished" somehow. What if Macy Chalmers was all alone? That might explain the terrible mistake she'd made in marrying an old man. There'd been no one to advise her differently. Dee winced, remembering the black underwear she'd come across in the girl's drawer, with the diary wrapped inside. "I don't like what's going on in that house," she said.

"What's going on?"

"You know what I mean, that man with that girl."

"So, quit."

"I told you, I promised Mrs. Chalmers to keep an eye on things. Besides, some of us need money to live on, or haven't you heard?"

"Ah, Dee, you could quit if you wanted to," he persisted. "You could quit all your fine ladies."

"And do what?"

"Come out to the country with me. Walk in the woods, pick the berries." He was lying in the recliner, his hand on his heart and a silly grin on his face that made her wonder if he wasn't partly serious. She hadn't thought of marrying Jot in ages, if marriage was what he meant. Not since Penny died—and Dee half blamed him for it—had the idea of living with him seriously crossed her mind. Jot wasn't husband material. She thought even the baby must have known that, sensed it somehow, along with her mother's distress over the fact, and that was why the child had chosen not to entrust herself to their uncertain care. Penny had faded before their eyes inside the plastic box with tubes where the doctors and nurses kept her; first she was blue, then pale yellow, and finally white. Through it all, her little face had been screwed up tight, like she was concentrating hard on death.

"Sorry, nature boy," Dee said. "If you want to go frisking in the woods, you'll have to get another playmate. Last time I checked, you didn't even have indoor plumbing."

"You ain't seen the place in so long, you might be surprised at what I got."

"I don't need your kind of surprises." She remembered once, years ago, waking up in his bed in the middle of the night; it had sounded as if someone in squeaky shoes was walking around on the cabin's roof. In the moonlight, she could make out tiny particles, like intermittent snow, falling toward them out of the darkness. She'd been afraid the ceiling was falling in. "Bats in the rafters," Jot told her, his voice husky and muffled, like a lover's.

"Nothing to worry about." She'd pushed him away from her—hard—and spent the rest of the night with her head under the blankets. "What's wrong, Dee?" she could hear him asking through the covers. "C'mon, tell me what's wrong."

DEE SO SELDOM laid eyes on Macy Chalmers she was surprised to walk in on her one Wednesday in the Chalmers' bedroom. The girl was on a step ladder trying to reach the tallest shelf of a bookcase. "Miss Plogger," she said, grasping one of the shelves to steady herself. "I didn't hear you."

Dee hesitated in the doorway. "I came to strip the bed." She knew the girl always changed the sheets herself.

"Come in, it's all right. I just didn't hear you."

It irritated Dee, her repeating this. Maybe Macy Chalmers thought she should wear a bell around her neck.

Dee started to turn back the bedspread. "Never mind about the sheets," the girl said. "But perhaps you could give me your opinion on something."

Dee looked up at her warily. She was standing at the very top of the ladder where it says not to, because it's not a step. The long toes of her bare feet curled around the edge of the ladder, gripping it as a monkey would. Having recovered her equilibrium now, she seemed sly like a monkey, too, looking down at Dee, one eye partially hidden behind strands of hair, as if she were peering through vines. "What do you think?" she said, gesturing toward the top shelf.

"Good lord," Dee said. The thing on the shelf was repulsive—a six-inch, dung-colored bust of an ugly old man. Or was it a bird, on account of its wings? Or a devil, because it had horns? The thing's face was roughly human, with big ears, nose, and mouth, but the slanted eyes, shadowed by prominent, arched brows, looked like a reptile's. The creature was leaning forward on its elbows, cupping its head in its hands. And it was sticking its tongue out! How insulting. Imagine bringing a thing like that into Evelyn Chalmers' house.

"David and I bought it in Mexico," the girl said. "As a sort of wedding present to ourselves."

"Wedding present!" Dee said. "It looks like something if you found it in your house you'd call the exterminator."

"It's supposed to look that way," the girl said defensively. "It's a gargoyle. They used to put them on churches to ward off evil spirits."

"I guess it's ugly enough to scare off most anything."

"You really think so?" Macy Chalmers looked pointedly at Dee. "You think it might keep away snoops?"

Dee wished later she'd thought to say, "And trespassers like you." But she didn't say anything. She just stood there, her face burning as if it had been slapped.

"Oh, well, I guess we'll leave it here for now," the girl said, coming down the ladder.

"I guess you can do whatever you want," the housekeeper muttered.

Dee considered giving her notice after that but knew if she did it would be taken as an admission she really had been snooping. How clever Macy Chalmers had been in accusing her without seeming to accuse her; anything Dee might have said by way of denial would only have ended up making her look more guilty. She wondered if the girl had confided her suspicions to David Chalmers or anyone else. Not that people in town who knew Dee would credit such a rumor, especially coming from the upstart Mrs. Chalmers. Still it galled her, even the possibility that her name might be sullied by this girl.

One thing for sure, she had no intention of setting foot in the Chalmers' bedroom again. But the following Wednesday, finding all her work finished early, she asked herself, what am I supposed to do, sit around and twiddle my thumbs? She was no sitter, she was a doer. Why not give the upstairs a dusting? "It's what I get paid for," she said aloud, though no one was around to hear her. A note left with her check that morning on the entrance hall table had informed her of the Chalmers' plans to be out of town for the day. "See you next week!" promised the exuberant scrawl at the bottom of the page.

Dee got a dust cloth from the broom closet, along with a stepladder to help her reach the high places. Climbing the main staircase, she thought she would not be ashamed for anyone in town to see her at this moment, doing what she was supposed to do, what she did better than anyone—keep house.

The work upstairs went quickly; after all, there was little dust to be found anywhere at the Chalmers', even by an eye as practiced as Dee's. She saved the master bedroom for last, nervous anticipation building in her as she worked her way toward it. "What is wrong with you?" she snapped at herself. All day she'd had the feeling of being watched, though she knew the house was empty. More than once she'd turned abruptly from some task, half expecting the girl to be standing there, smirking at her from behind that curtain of hair. That awful hair! How Dee would have liked to take scissors and whack it off. How she would have relished the naked and startled expression on Macy Chalmers' face. No more hiding then. Eye-to-eye, let them have it out.

When she reached the bedroom she pocketed her dust cloth, left the stepladder at the door, and went right to the girl's dresser. She kneeled down and took hold of the knobs of the bottom drawer. She paused, thinking, not for the first time in her private visits to this part of the house, it's as still as a tomb in here; thinking, what am I then, some kind of grave robber?

That was ridiculous, of course. She had no intention of taking anything. She only wanted to look at the diary, reassure herself it was still there. It had been in the back of her mind to do just that the week before when she'd walked in on Macy Chalmers. The diary drew her irresistibly with its promise of secrets revealed. Dee had never kept such a book herself as a girl. In a family of eight children, concealment was out of the question. Besides, she'd always tended to think of her own life as more or less an open book. The idea of a solitary child writing things down, then hiding them away, seemed peculiar to her, almost like the custom of some foreign land. What might such a book contain?

Her hands trembled so as she fumbled through the drawer she could scarcely believe they belonged to her. She watched with distaste as the hands hurried on to the next drawer, and the next, sifting and searching, though by now she knew it was useless. The diary wasn't there. She shoved the last drawer closed. The girl had tricked her, hidden the book someplace beyond finding this time, no doubt.

She glanced up at the top shelf of the bookcase where the Chalmers' wedding present to each other, the creature with wings and horns, and a protruding tongue, leered at her through the late afternoon dusk. Hateful thing! She thought it looked a little like old David Chalmers himself. Dee wadded up the dust cloth in her pocket and flung it at the statue. To her amazement, she hit it; the thing tottered and fell on its side, the head rolling free.

She retrieved the stepladder from the doorway and climbed up to examine the damage. Her heart was knocking against her ribs and she had to hold onto the shelves to keep from falling. The statue was broken in three pieces—body, head, and nose—not to mention several powdery chips and fragments scattered about.

"Now you've gone and done it," said a voice inside her head. It was the voice of calamity and sounded remarkably like Jot Dooley.

"Be quiet, you," she hissed. "I've got to think."

EVELYN CHALMERS USED to say, in happier times, that she owed her marriage to glue. Once she'd broken an antique soup tureen belonging to David's mother. "You know the one I mean, Dee—only the most valuable piece of china in the whole house!" Though Evelyn took considerable pains mending it, there was no way, she feared, her husband would fail to notice the damage to this heirloom. "Dee, weeks passed and he never said a word! After a while, I got cocky and started serving soups and stews out of that tureen, right under the man's nose. Not once did he so much as look cross-eyed at his mother's precious bowl."

Dee wasn't so sure glue was the way out of her own predicament; it was easier to fool a man than his sharp-sighted young wife. But what other choice did she have? Macy Chalmers would never have believed her if she claimed the statue was broken in a dusting mishap, not after the words they'd had over it the week before. Dee thought the cracks in the gargoyle were undetectable if you weren't looking for them, but she reminded herself the girl had discovered her earlier forays into the bedroom on even less evidence—on no evidence at all really, since Dee had always been careful to leave things exactly as she found them.

The following Wednesday she arrived at the Chalmers' earlier than usual, hoping to slip in and get to work before anyone noticed she was there. Work made her strong and if there was going to be a scene she'd feel more secure playing her part with a mop or a dishrag in hand. The girl, however, was already in the kitchen when she walked in. "Miss Plogger, I've made coffee, would you like some?"

"I don't drink it." Dee thought this sounded a little abrupt. "Not anymore, that is. Makes me tender." She trailed a hand across her chest. "Through here, you know."

"I'm sorry."

"No need to be sorry, I don't miss it a bit." She was proud of having given up coffee, like card playing before that; these two were practically the last of her vices. Unlike Jot and others she knew, Dee had no intention of going through middle age as a slave to bad habits.

"I'm not much of a coffee drinker myself," said Macy Chalmers. "But it was so cold in the house this morning I thought it would taste good."

"Winter's not far off, that's true."

"Oh, don't say it! I'm not ready for winter yet."

Maybe you would be, Dee thought, if you put on some clothes. The girl's teats were standing out against her thin t-shirt, and the housekeeper averted her eyes so as not to appear to be staring. She pictured old David Chalmers lying upstairs in his bed that was probably still warm from this girl being in it. If you asked Dee, there were plenty of crimes that were not against the law—but should be.

She felt too relieved on her own behalf that morning, however, to brood on the offenses of others. Nothing said about the statue! Maybe the girl wasn't so smart after all. Or maybe Evelyn Chalmers had been looking out for Dee, guiding her in the right direction. ("Glue. Trust me.") The housekeeper felt a pang of loneliness for her former employer and would have liked to share with her the story of how the new wife had been tricked.

The day was nearly over when Macy Chalmers poked her head in the parlor where Dee was running the vacuum. "Miss Plogger, would you mind very much changing the sheets upstairs? I didn't get around to it this week." It was the first request the girl had ever made of her, and even then, Dee noted, with a disapproving glance at her watch, it had taken her nearly all day to think of it. "I really would appreciate it," the girl added. Beneath the beholden manner, she seemed actually to be insisting.

"I'll see what I can do." Dee didn't want to go upstairs. Except for a quick check of the bathrooms that morning, she'd avoided doing so. She particularly did not want to revisit the scene of last week's misadventure. But neither did she want to spend another week wondering if she'd been found out.

As she headed up the winding stairs through the gathering shadows, she felt as if Evelyn Chalmers' house, which she knew almost as well as her own, had turned against her and was a giant trap set to spring. At the center of the trap lay the bedroom which had proved such an irresistible temptation to her, but which she now entered with as much dread as curiosity. And with good reason, for Macy Chalmers had obviously decided to dispel any doubts her housekeeper might have had about the success of her experiment with glue. The wedding present which Dee had broken, then carefully put back together, now lay on the top bookshelf, dismembered once again—body, head, and nose.

By this dumb show, Dee understood the girl to speak quite plainly, even bluntly: I know what you did, and now you know I know.

Dee left the Chalmers' that day without picking up her check, left so fast she almost knocked over old David Chalmers, who was coming up the front porch stairs. The polished walking stick he carried—one of the man's affectations—slipped from his grasp in the collision and clattered down the steps. "Miss Plogger," he called after her, "is everything all right?"

Her check arrived in the mail two days later without comment, except for the girl's usual "Thank You!" on the memo line. What did it mean? Why didn't Macy Chalmers say she was fired? Was she waiting for Dee to admit her mistake and ask pardon? She likes lording it over me, the housekeeper thought. She wants to make me squirm. Dee had had enough of this girl's furtive games. She'd been lured into acting against her character and she'd been humiliated. Now she was through with David and Macy Chalmers. If either of them called to ask what had happened to her, she would know what to say. She practiced it, a little speech about loyalty to a former employer and friend, a few well-chosen words about the impossibility of continuing to work in the house Mrs. Chalmers had been forced to leave. That would put the newlyweds in their place and also remind them indirectly just how minor Dee's transgressions were compared to their own.

But no one called. Maybe the girl was as relieved to be rid of her as she was to be gone. Except Dee wasn't relieved. She couldn't shake the feeling she'd behaved shamefully. In spite of this, or maybe because of it, she hated Macy Chalmers. When *The Weekly Gazette* printed a picture of "Mrs. David L. Chalmers" at a wine-tasting party, standing with no less a person than "Mrs. Hartley A. Matthews," one of Dee's ladies, it was almost more than the housekeeper could bear, seeing her enemy thus exalted. In the photograph the girl wore pearls and earrings; her hair was pulled into a knot so her face was plainly visible for a change. Her head was tipped back, revealing the fine line of her chin and the top row of her small, white teeth. She was laughing, apparently at something Mrs. Hartley Matthews had said. Dee looked and looked at the picture, disturbed and fascinated by it at the same time. Among other things, the photograph raised questions about the girl's acceptance into the community. Dee had supposed she was being routinely snubbed, but obviously that was not so. She felt like writing Evelyn Chalmers to let her know who her real friends were but refrained from doing so lest she add to that poor lady's grievances.

In the meantime Dee consoled herself with the knowledge she'd have no trouble getting work to replace what she'd lost. When word got around she had a day free, one or more of her ladies would surely want it or they would know someone who did. Several weeks passed, however, and no one claimed Wednesday. Dee was incredulous at first, then suspicious. She'd been stingy in reporting the details of her separation from the Chalmers, and maybe that had been her mistake; it gave the girl a chance to spread her own version of events and so undermine her. On one occasion she happened to speak slightingly of Macy Chalmers in the presence of her Thursday lady, and that woman threw up her hand like a traffic cop. "Really, Dee," she said somewhat coldly, "I don't feel comfortable being drawn into your feud with the Chalmers."

Her feud? Dee wanted to ask when it had become hers alone, wanted to inquire exactly when this betrayal of Evelyn Chalmers by her old friends had taken place and Evelyn's enemies had stopped being theirs. She kept quiet though, afraid to lose Thursday now that Wednesday had gone begging. Already the middle of the week yawned for her like a chasm. She felt as if this girl—it was all Macy Chalmers' fault—had hounded her to the brink of some personal disaster she was powerless to avoid.

JOT CAUGHT HER at home one Wednesday. "I seen your car in the drive," he said. "You sick, Dee?" He knew she'd quit the Chalmers, though not the real reason. Also Dee had kept from him the fact she'd been unable to find other work.

"Do I look sick?"

He took the question seriously, studying her.

"I'm not sick," she said.

"So what's going on?"

"I'm taking the day off."

"C'mon!"

"Why not?"

"You?"

"I'm entitled."

"Well, sure." His puzzlement relaxed into a loose grin. "So Dee Plogger's playing hooky."

"Not hooky." She glared at him. "That's you."

"Don't get mad," he said. "C'mon, I'll buy you a burger and Coke."

It was a crisp winter day with the sun low in the sky. The mountains on the horizon were gun-metal gray and Jot, who'd served in the Navy, said they reminded him of big ships lifting their prows. He tapped the wheel and whistled as he drove. He said he was taking her on a picnic, he had a spot in mind. But after they got the hamburgers, she told him, "I want to go to the cemetery."

"What for?"

"Take me back to the house first," she said. "I want to get some things to clean Penny's gravestone. I'm sure it needs it." She'd been thinking of their daughter more and more these days, thinking of her in the cemetery alone. Odd, because she never used to picture her in that place before, which was why she'd rarely bothered to visit. Now she was feeling a little guilty for all the years of neglect. "C'mon," she said, "turn around."

"Can't you ever just relax? Leave things be?"

"No."

"Well, we're not going to the cemetery." He hunched over the steering wheel, eyes straight ahead.

"Stop the truck and let me out then."

"Listen. We're not going because the gravestone's fine. It don't need cleaning."

"How would you know?"

He looked at her, exasperated. "Because I go there sometimes. I know it's all right."

"*You* do? Penny's grave?" After a long silence, she said, "I don't think I've ever heard you even speak that child's name."

His head sunk a little on his shoulders, like he was trying to pull it in. "I guess I say it—to myself sometimes."

They kept going toward the mountains he'd said were like ships. Dee couldn't get over his visiting their daughter's grave. To think that all along, of the two of them, he'd been the more faithful parent.

They turned onto a gravel road. "I know where you're taking me," she said.

"Just wait a minute." They drove down a dirt path, through a ravine, and up a hill. Jot steered the truck through some trees and out onto the top of the hill; coming into the clear, it was like a curtain parting—all sky and mountains. Down at the foot of the hill was his cabin, but not as she remembered it. There was a new porch on the front, for sitting. And the chimney looked different, too. "Rebricked and painted," Jot said. The whole house had been spruced up. Were those curtains at the windows?

He sat there grinning at her, waiting for her to say something, but she didn't know what to say. For the second time this afternoon, he'd taken her by surprise. "C'mon, let's walk down," he said. "I'll show you the inside."

"No," she said. "It's pretty, really. But I—" It upset her that the cabin was changed. It seemed to suggest he'd changed, too. Sometime when she wasn't looking, he'd become a man who visited his daughter's grave and undertook home improvements. "Let's just sit here."

"Okay." He slid over next to her.

"You're squashing the burgers," she said.

"So?"

"What's got into you?"

"You smell like moth balls," he said, sniffing at her shoulder.

"Get away, you."

"Don't take it wrong," he said. "I like it. It smells clean—like you." And he beamed at her, as if he were proud of thinking up such a compliment.

IT WAS FROM her Monday lady that she first learned of Evelyn Chalmers' death in Florida. "Dee, this is the terrible part. They think she may have killed herself." Evelyn had been found drowned—floating in a canal behind her sister's house. "The sister says they were lucky to recover the body at all," Dee's lady told her, aghast. "Those canals are full of alligators."

"You better stop," Dee said sternly, thinking she'd have to put the woman to bed if she were permitted to torment herself with grisly details. One detail, however, haunted the housekeeper herself. She couldn't put out of her head the picture of Mrs. Chalmers floating on the water—just floating, waiting to be discovered; it seemed such a pointless end to a life Dee had always

considered more purposeful than most. She'd never known anyone more strong-willed and clear-headed than her former
employer. Or more dignified. Poor Mrs. Chalmers. Fished out of
a canal! This was the cold fact that stuck with Dee in the following days, as additional bits of information made their way up
from Florida. Evelyn's health, it was reported, had grown steadily worse in the weeks before her death; so, too, the bouts of
depression from which she was said to have suffered. Her sister,
besides, was judged to be a stingy, unwelcoming person who'd
invited Evelyn to live with her less from a desire for companionship than extra income.

Such "explanations" for what had happened made Dee
seethe. People mouthed them, she believed, merely out of con-
venience, because it was easier than denouncing the real cul-
prits, who were uncomfortably near at hand, residing happily in
the dead woman's house.

Then another piece of news came from Florida. By a provi-
sion of Evelyn's will, she was to be buried here, in the town
where she'd lived for more than thirty years. So, Dee thought,
the poor drowned body would not be allowed simply to disappear, after all; it was to be washed up on their very doorsteps, and
on the doorstep of David and Macy Chalmers in particular.
Good. They were all to be made witnesses, required to look at it.

No sooner had word of this development begun to spread
than David Chalmers phoned Dee to ask if she could help out in
the house on the day of the funeral; his daughters with their fam-
ilies were coming from out of town; other relatives and close
friends were expected as well. There was no mention of the trouble Dee'd had with his young wife. "I know it would please
Evelyn to have you here again," he said, when she agreed to
come. "She always said there was no one she trusted more to take
care of the house." The man sounded chastened—all the old
coot foolishness gone out of him; his voice came through distant
and hollow, as if he were speaking from the bottom of a deep

hole; as if Evelyn's death had pushed him suddenly into the company of his own mortality. Never mind the girl he'd been trying to cheat time and nature with.

"THANK GOD, IT'S you, Dee," said her Thursday lady, meeting her at the Chalmers' front door. "Nobody seems to know where anything is around here. People have been bringing food—you wouldn't believe how much food!—and it's all just piling up in the kitchen."

"Where's the wife?" Dee said. She would never be able to call that girl "Mrs. Chalmers," least of all today.

The Thursday lady pulled a face. "That's the mystery of the hour. I haven't seen her. The Chalmers' daughters are here, of course, but they've got their hands full with their father." The lady leaned close, touching Dee's arm, and said, with a note of triumph even her whisper couldn't diminish, "The man is stricken. Absolutely stricken."

On her way to the kitchen, Dee hesitated at the parlor door, peeking in, half expecting to find a coffin with the body in it, though she knew better; not even country people buried loved ones from their homes anymore. Still, death was in the house. You could hear it in the subdued voices of those who'd come to pay their respects. You could see it in the way the women clustered in corners and the men kept to the fringes of rooms, their shoulders and backs almost brushing the flocked wallpaper. Evelyn Chalmers had returned—to her house; she was a formidable presence within these walls, and the mourners seemed unconsciously to be making way for her.

The exception was the kitchen, where some of the women had congregated in hopes of being useful. All was commotion there. Dee's Thursday lady began shooing them out. "Miss Plogger's here now." A few protested their expulsion, but Dee stood stolidly in the middle of the room, still wearing her coat and holding her pocketbook, making clear she would not get down to business until everyone else had retired. "All right, I'm leaving, too," sighed her Thursday lady, seeing no exception was to be made for her.

The kitchen counters were crammed with covered dishes and desserts, but people had neglected as usual to bring breads, rolls, and biscuits, which Dee considered the most consoling foods at times like these. Resolving to throw together some biscuits, she went into the pantry to look for the ingredients. The room, which opened off the back of the kitchen, was L-shaped, lined from floor to ceiling with canned goods and sundries. "Please, don't come back here," a voice said from around the corner of the L. Dee stopped. It was Macy Chalmers' voice. What was she doing back here? The housekeeper started around the corner but the girl pushed by her, emitting a little cry, and would have gotten away, too, except a noise in the kitchen cut short her escape.

"Dee?" It was the Thursday lady again. "Oh, there you are. Here's more food, I'm afraid. Say, are you sure you don't want some help?"

Dee said she was sure. "I can work faster alone."

Returning to the pantry, she thought the girl looked as if she might still bolt. "I didn't let on you were here," the housekeeper said, keeping between her and the pantry exit. Macy Chalmers shrugged. Like the brilliant red lips she'd painted on her otherwise waxen face, the shrug seemed to be a way of denying her predicament. Maybe she read in her former housekeeper's expression just how feeble a bluff it was. Or maybe the fact that here she was hiding out in her own pantry persuaded her to drop the pretense. "Why can't you leave me alone?" she said. It was like the complaint of a harried child and probably not meant all that personally, but Dee took it that way, feeling it in her chest, as if Macy Chalmers had put the heel of her hand there and shoved her away. Not that she didn't deserve it. Why did she always find herself intruding on this girl's privacy?

"I'm sorry," Dee said. It was not the sort of thing she'd ever imagined telling Macy Chalmers.

The girl stared at her, something dangerously wild in her aspect. "I hate this house," she said. "There's nowhere for me to be in it."

The vehemence of the words shocked Dee. She'd always assumed Macy Chalmers counted herself fortunate to be the mistress of this place. Why else had she taken such fastidious care of it, hardly needing a housekeeper at all? Why else had she kept everything almost exactly as Mrs. Chalmers left it? Unless the girl felt her predecessor never really had left, that she was still here, present in every household particular that bore her stamp, right down to the yellow, pleated shade that made a little Chinaman's hat for the pantry bulb dangling above their heads. What if Macy Chalmers had turned caretaker not from pride of occupancy but fear of reproach? If so, it must have been like living in a museum—or worse. What had David Chalmers called the place on that first day back from his honeymoon, the morning he introduced his bride to Dee? A mausoleum.

You poor, trapped thing, Dee thought. "Listen," she said, her voice low and urgent, like a conspirator's, "wouldn't you like to get out of here for a little while?"

The housekeeper had no idea where she was taking the girl as she led the way out the back door and down the long sloping driveway to Thorn Hill Street. Nor did she have any confidence Macy Chalmers would actually follow her. She kept glancing over her shoulder to make sure she was there. When they were seated in the car, an immaculate beige Plymouth Dee had bought at a bargain some years ago from one of her ladies, Dee remembered her coat back at the house and her pocketbook with the keys in it. "Wait here," she told Macy. Two old men stood smoking on the Chalmers' front porch, solemnly watching the housekeeper retrace her steps. She hadn't noticed them there before. One of the men raised his hand in greeting but she ignored him.

Back in the kitchen her Thursday lady was standing amidst the food looking perplexed. "Dee?"

"I forgot my coat and pocketbook."

"But—"

"Mrs. Chalmers and I are going out for something," the housekeeper said. "You'll have to take over for a while."

Dee didn't look back at the house as she hurried down the Chalmers' drive a second time and across the street to her car. She didn't need to look, sensing the witnesses to her departure numbered more than the two old smokers this time. Sure enough, when she got in the car—the girl's eyes were closed, her head tilted back against the seat—Dee glanced up toward the porch where several people, including two or three of her ladies, were all gazing intently into the street. One of the women came part way down the stairs and called to her. "Miss Plogger! Dee!"

Macy Chalmers moaned softly. The housekeeper showed a stern face to the woman on the steps, emphatically applying a finger to her lips. Then she turned quickly to check on the girl, whose presence, here beside her, she could scarcely believe in even now.

ETHER

rank kicked the back of the desk with his clodhopper, but all the girl did was turn half around in her seat and give him a sad smile that made him want to kick her again. This was their day to feel sorry for him.

"Class," Mrs. Toms had said first thing that morning, "we are going to be losing one of our members today. Frank's mother will be coming after lunch to take him to the hospital." Their big, solemn eyes were on him at once. "Frank is going to have his feet operated on," Mrs. Toms explained. Their eyes all genuflected toward the clodhoppers.

"The operation's not going to hurt or anything," he told them.

"Of course not," Mrs. Toms said. "And next year when Frank comes back to school, he'll be able to run as fast as any of you."

Faster, Frank thought. Dr. Pipken had shown him the photographs of other boys whose fallen arches he'd fixed better than new, boys in cleats and sneakers, posed dashingly in their team uniforms.

"Poor Frank!" erupted Michelle Miller from the front of the room. She was every year the class UNICEF representative and was given to spasms of grief and sympathy. Also she and Frank had a history. Michelle chased the boys to kiss them, and for more than a year now plodding Frank—to his shame— had known her sweet, sticky lips better than any boy in the third grade.

It galled Frank that a day he'd so looked forward to was taking this somber turn. He'd wanted to point out to them he was getting out of the last two weeks of school for this. He'd wanted to tell them about the big plans he had for his hospital stay. How his father had sent him a model of the USS Yorktown, an exact replica of the World War II aircraft carrier his dad had served on. How the model came in a cellophane wrapped box almost as big as a suitcase, with over three hundred pieces, including gun turrets that moved. And how he was going to put this together all by himself as he lay in bed watching remote control TV and being waited on by nurses. And mostly he had wanted to tell them—as his mother had told him—about the ether that made it all so painless and nice. How it smelled like cotton candy and would put him to sleep before he could count to ten.

But he hadn't gotten to tell them any of these things. He kicked the desk in front of him, harder this time, and the girl straightened and gave a satisfying little gasp. Mrs. Toms came and stood over Frank. She put a book down in front of him and tapped its hard cover with her fingernail. It was the quiet time after lunch, and they were supposed to be either reading or resting their heads on their desks.

Just then there was a clicking of heels and a rustling of taffeta outside the door and in swept Frank's mother in a pink sheath and matching shoes, with Mr. Reeky, the principal, trailing.

"We've come for young Francis," announced Mr. Reeky, a little out of breath.

"Frank," Frank's mother corrected him.

"Of course," said the principal. "Frank." Mr. Reeky was shorter than Frank's mother. "Is he ready, Mrs. Toms? I'm told they must be going."

Mrs. Toms made her way deliberately to the front of the room. "Children," she said, because they were all buzzing over Frank's mother, whom most of them had never seen.

"She's beautiful," one little girl gushed. "Frank, your mom's beautiful."

"She looks just like Dinah Shore," Michelle Miller said.

"Children!" said Mrs. Toms, who had once been declared the prettiest teacher in the school by Michelle Miller but had never, Frank was certain, been compared to anyone on TV. "Children!"

Frank's mother beckoned, and he got up and went to her without waiting for Mrs. Toms' permission. His mother brushed his cheek with her hand, then took him by the shoulders and turned him so he was facing the class. The white arm she draped across his chest had a sweet, heavy fragrance, like the lilacs in his grandfather's yard that always made him feel pleasantly drowsy.

Nobody was looking at the clodhoppers now. Michelle Miller stared up at Frank and his mother with her mouth open, a tiny piece of hard candy glinting like an emerald on her tongue. Frank thought of the story Mrs. Toms had read them about the toad that swallowed a precious jewel and had to be charmed by the princess to give it up. Michelle looked as if she would gladly give up her candy just to trade places with Frank. She'd forgotten all about the operation. The whole class had.

"We've planned a farewell ceremony," Mrs. Toms said.

Two children came forward and read alternate verses on a card the teacher had picked out and they had all signed when Frank wasn't looking. It was about friendship, and before they finished, Michelle Miller had recovered her senses and was blubbering. It was even worse than usual. "Hush, child," said Mr. Reeky, venturing to stroke Michelle's hair. She only got louder. Frank felt his mother's arm tighten across his chest. A few other girls started to sniffle.

"Children!" said Mrs. Toms. Some of the boys had started to mimic the girls and were even outdoing them, bawling louder than Michelle herself. There had not been such lamentation since the class fish went belly up in his tank. "Maybe the child doesn't feel well," said Frank's mother, referring to Michelle. "She should go to the nurse." "Nonsense," Mrs. Toms said, in a way that reminded Frank his teacher and his mother didn't get along. They had disagreed once over a piece of birthday cake. Frank had refused the cake on the grounds he'd given up sweets for Lent, and Mrs. Toms, who didn't like being balked in her own classroom, and was a Baptist besides, had made mild fun of him in front of the others. Frank's mother, when she learned of it, called the teacher at home. "You know what that woman had the nerve to say to me?" Frank overheard his mother tell his grandfather afterwards. "She said, 'It's a good thing the Pope isn't running the country yet, that's all I have to say.' She's probably afraid there's going to be an inquisition if Kennedy's elected. I told her, 'I am ashamed of you, Mrs. Toms, a teacher, making a remark like that. I only hope your prejudice is not influencing the children in your care.' Oh, I was so mad. But I took the high ground with her, Papa. I do believe the old Republican was ashamed of herself, too, by the time I got through with her." Two days later Frank was sent to school with a bag of JFK buttons his mother had gotten through her boss, and Mrs. Toms watched stonily from the foot of the flagpole as he passed them out at recess.

At last Mrs. Toms was able to stop the crying of Michelle and the others by threatening to take away their afternoon snack. When they were all quiet, Frank's mother made a speech, thanking the class for the card they'd given Frank and for being such good friends to him. She hoped they would visit him when he got home from the hospital. "Frank is going to be quite the man of leisure this summer, and I know he'd appreciate some company."

"We're getting a 22-inch TV," Frank told them.

"I'm coming," said one of the boys.

"Good," Frank's mother said. "I've got a whole freezer full of Eskimo Pies and Popsicles. You can help Frank eat them."

"I'll help, too."

"Me, too."

"We've got all sorts of games," Frank said, as his mother eased him toward the door. Mr. Reeky was holding it open, smiling broadly.

"When can we come?"

"Anytime."

"Yea, Frank!"

"Bye, Frank!"

"Lucky dog."

Escorted by his mother and the principal, Frank made his way toward the bright spring day framed like a picture in the big glass door at the end of the hall. Behind him Mrs. Toms' tired voice rose above the giddy din. "Calm down," she was saying, "calm down now. It's lesson time."

THEY MADE FIFTEEN lights in a row on their way to the hospital. If one turned red as they were approaching, Frank's mother would slow down until they were barely creeping along, holding their breath for the light to change. Then at what always seemed the last second, it would change and they would go shooting through the intersection with a cheer. "We must be living right," Frank's mother said.

Finally a red light just over the crest of a hill surprised them and they had no choice but to stop. Some negro men were standing on the corner, brown paper bags with twisted necks dangling from their hands. The bags reminded Frank of dead chickens he'd seen on his father's farm. The neighborhood, too, reminded him of his father. He was sure they had driven through here the time they went to see the A's play. His father gave some money to a man like one of those on the corner to watch his car. It was dark then, but Frank didn't remember being afraid.

"Keep your eyes straight ahead," his mother said. "Is your door locked?"

Frank slid his arm up over the window sill, feeling for the button with his elbow. The light took a long time to change.

Then they were off again, swinging onto one of the city's old tree-lined boulevards that would take them right to the front of St. Joseph's Hospital, where Frank had been born and where now he was about to become a man of leisure. He jiggled the big box on his lap, delighting in the muffled rattle of the USS Yorktown's hundreds of parts.

"I hope you're not going to be disappointed," his mother said. She had earlier shown him the place on the box where it said "Recommended for Age 12 and Up." Frank wasn't worried. He'd done planes and cars and small boats. He was sure he was ready for this aircraft carrier. It was what he looked forward to most about his stay in the hospital—watching the big boat slowly take shape under his skilled hands.

"What did your dad say when he called last night?" his mother asked.

"He said, 'How's your coperatus seem to graduate?'"

"He always says that."

"Yeah. Mom, what does it mean?"

"I don't know, it's just a silly thing." Then she added, "Your dad loves you, you know that?"

Yes, Frank supposed he knew that. Not that it was much on his mind. He had his mother for the whole afternoon. Her boss, Mr. Horgan, had given her the rest of the day off. What else could he do? She typed one hundred fifty words a minute without an error, so naturally he did what he could to make sure she was content. Mr. Horgan kept Frank's mother in a frosted glass enclosure, away from the other secretaries, and once he'd told her with tears in his eyes that she was like the daughter he never had. Frank's mother used to say of her job, "It's nice to be appreciated."

Frank suspected his father's big mistake had been in failing to appreciate his mother. Somehow his father had missed her fineness or had decided to ignore it. Why else would he take her from her father's home in the city where she was happy to Buckner, Missouri, where he'd tried to make a farm wife of her? "Mud and molting chickens," that was how Frank's mother remembered Buckner. Even now she had only to hear the name Buckner and a shudder would pass over her.

AFTER FRANK WAS checked into the hospital and settled in his bed, the first thing his roommate, Bucky, told him was he should ask the doctor for Sodium Pentothal, not ether.

"Why?"

"With ether you puke your guts out."

"That's not true."

"I'm telling you, Sodium Pentothal's what I had. It doesn't make you sick. You just say things while you're going under. It's like truth serum."

Bucky was recovering from a tonsillectomy but seemed to be feeling no pain. He had a strawberry milkshake on the tray beside his bed and, in his lap, a jar with the parts they'd cut out of him floating in a solution. "The big ones are the tonsils," he explained to Frank, holding the jar up and revolving it in his hands. "The little ones are the adenoids."

Frank only pretended to look. He couldn't imagine wanting to save his clodhoppers after the operation. His mother didn't like him to call the shoes clodhoppers. She called them "orthopedic." But his father, who wore similar shoes on the farm, had always referred to them as clodhoppers. Michelle Miller had another name for them; she called them "Lil' Abners," after the comic-strip hillbilly whose shoes were as big as anvils.

Bucky wore a Yankees cap with a crease in the crown and a curved bill that hugged his temples. He had a deck of baseball cards that he would shuffle and reshuffle, sometimes dispatching them to positions on his bed, as if the bed were a ball field and the colorful fraternity of players, brandishing their bats and flashing their grins, had congregated for no other purpose than to do his bidding. Occasionally he would take a draw on his milkshake. Or he would lean back and look up at the TV through half-closed eyes, whistling softly between his teeth, as if he weren't really paying attention. To Frank he was the image of masculine repose.

Frank's mother had gone to see about a television for him. In the meantime he decided to remove the cellophane wrapper from the USS Yorktown and have a look inside. Studying the picture of the completed boat on the front of the box had not prepared him for the sheer number and intricacy of its parts. Bucky reached across and snatched the instructions; he gave them a shake and Frank watched as they unfurled all the way to the floor. "Geez, kid, how long did you say you're in here for?"

"Give them back."

"Sure, but I think you'd better call the Navy to help you put it together."

When Frank's mother returned, she had Dr. Pipken with her. "You let me handle that," the doctor was saying as they came in.

"I just thought—"

"You think too much," he told her.

"Hi, sweetie," Frank's mother said, with exaggerated gaiety.

"Hey, pal," said Dr. Pipken, sweeping back the sheet and grabbing up one of Frank's feet for inspection. He was the most brilliant surgeon in the city, according to Frank's mother. Because of this she was willing to put up with his discourtesy.

Frank liked him, this tall, rumpled man with horn-rimmed glasses. He even liked the brusque manner; it gave him confidence. He always tried to keep his mouth shut and not complain around the doctor. He tried to be a boy with spunk because he could tell that's what Dr. Pipken would admire.

"How fast did you say they timed you in the 35-yard dash?" the doctor asked.

"Seven-five," Frank said softly, ashamed for Bucky to hear.

"Listen to me, son," he said, leaning close to Frank as he replaced the sheet. "Next year at this time you'll do five-five."

"Did you hear that, Frank?" said his mother.

"Get your sleep tonight," Dr. Pipken said. "You and I have a day ahead of us tomorrow."

Frank's father called after dinner. His mother answered the phone. "We're as cozy as can be," she told him. "Just the two of us." She had discovered a cord that, when pulled, caused a curtain to surround the bed.

"It's like being inside a tent," Frank explained to his father. "Only we've got television."

"If you were in a tent down here today," his father said, "you'd get swamped. Can you hear the thunder?"

He thought he could. "It's storming bad in Buckner," Frank told his mother.

"Tell him he'd better go down in the cellar."

"Can't," Frank's father said. "Water in the cellar. Electricity's out, too. I'm sitting here in the dark." He sounded almost cheerful.

"Oh, look, Frank," his mother said. *The Ann Sothern Show* was coming on. It was one of her favorites.

His father's voice boomed into his ear, above the thunder and the static on the line: "It rained so hard one of the cows got herself stuck in the creek bed. She like to drowned. Had to pull her out with the tractor."

"Is that true?" Frank thought of Paul Bunyan and his blue ox. His father, too, performed impossible feats.

"So, how's your coperatus seem to graduate?"

"Great." He was looking at the TV. Ann Sothern was tripping down a city street in a polka dot raincoat, twirling an umbrella. She wore a tam cocked at a jaunty angle on her blonde head. "Dad? It says on the box the USS Yorktown is for age twelve and up."

"You can do it," his father said. "It may take a while, but you're good with your hands, like me."

"Okay."

"You're not just any nine year old. You're smarter than most. You know how to figure things out."

"I know."

"That's what I'm counting on," his father said.

Up on the screen, the wind turned Ann Sothern's umbrella inside out and blew the tam from her head. The hat didn't get far though. An old gentleman rescued it. He drove a horse and carriage, and he invited Ann to get in, out of the elements. She did, and they rode off together, Ann smiling and waving at the pedestrians, like she was in a parade.

Frank and his mother watched TV until a hand parted the curtain and a nun who was also a nurse came and stood inside their tent. She wore a big, black rosary around her ample middle, with a crucifix dangling in front. Her thumbs were hooked in the rosary as if it were a gunbelt and she were the marshal. "Young lady," she said to Frank's mother, "the visiting period has been over for almost an hour."

"My son is having surgery tomorrow," Frank's mother said, not budging from the side of the bed where she was sitting. "Please, give us a minute."

After the nun went out, they watched television a little longer, then Frank's mother told him to turn it off. "Don't forget to say your prayers," she said, hugging him close. The familiar scent of lilacs washed over him and he clutched at her. "Ask Virgin Mary to be with you," she said, "and you won't be afraid."

"Mom," he whispered, "is it true that ether makes you sick?"

"Would Dr. Pipken give you something that made you sick? Would I let him?"

"Bucky said—"

"Remember how you used to fall asleep in the back seat at the drive-in movie? It was such a deep sleep you could never remember anything about the trip home or about your father carrying you into the house. All you knew was, next morning, there you were safe and snug in your bed. That's how it's going to be with the ether, only this time when you wake up you're going to have nice, springy arches in those feet."

"Don't believe her, kid," Bucky said, after Frank's mother had gone. "She'll say anything to keep her baby from being scared."

"Shut up," Frank said.

"It's your funeral."

Speaking of funerals, Bucky wanted to know if Frank had heard about the catacombs that lay beneath the hospital. He said the catacombs had first been constructed as a bomb shelter but now the Catholics buried their dead nuns and priests down there. Also it was where they kept the patients they managed to kill. "It's pretty terrible, kid. They wrap the bodies up in bandages from head to toe, say some mumbo jumbo over them, then just prop them up against the walls, like mummies. You can hardly breathe down there, it smells so bad."

"Oh, sure," Frank said. He didn't know what catacombs were, but as a student of the public schools he'd often heard superstitious stories about Catholics and had learned to ignore them. "It's a waste of time trying to explain the truth to some people," his mother said. It was her theory that nine out of ten times such people were either Baptists or Republicans. Frank wondered if Bucky were one or the other of these, or both, like Mrs. Toms.

Frank's father was both, or had been raised both. He practiced neither creed now. Frank's mother still prayed for his conversion to Catholicism. Not that she hoped this would lead to a reconciliation between them. She'd told Frank that she and his father, though they had not been divorced, would never again live together. But that didn't mean she wished him ill. In fact, she trusted they would all some day be united in heaven, where everything that had been clouded here on earth would come clear.

Frank couldn't go to sleep. For one thing, Bucky snored. He snored almost as loudly as Frank's grandfather, who had blocked sinuses. Sometimes his grandfather's snoring would get so loud that Frank's mother would go in and shake the old man. "Papa, you're doing it again." He would smile benignly, roll over, and usually stop. Even in sleep he did his best to please Frank's mother.

Frank decided to try his mother's approach with Bucky. He got out of bed, went over to the other boy, and gently shook him by the shoulder. Bucky sat bolt upright, his eyes wild and uncomprehending, his chin wet with drool. His Yankees cap had been knocked bill-sidewise in his sleep. Frank couldn't help but smile. Bucky looked like an idiot child. "You were snoring," he said, trying to stifle a giggle.

"What?"

"You were snoring, I couldn't sleep."

Bucky's eyes narrowed and focused on Frank. "Hey, I was asleep!"

"I'm sorry, you were snoring."

"Couldn't be. No adenoids."

"Sorry."

Bucky said, "If you wake me up again, I'll punch you in the face." Then he rolled over and went back to sleep.

Frank returned to his bed, shaken by the threat. He pressed the button for the nurse. "I can't go to sleep," he told her.

"You aren't trying." It was the nun who'd sent his mother away.

"What's wrong?" Another nun had come in behind her. They looked ghostly in their flowing white robes, and Frank wondered if they stayed in the catacombs when they weren't up here among the living.

"I'm scared," he said.

"There, there," said the first nun, rubbing his back.

"I suppose this is the one with the mother," said the second nun. "You guessed it," said the first.

FRANK WAS IN and out of sleep the next morning as they rolled him down the dim, undulant passageways toward the place where Dr. Pipken was waiting for him. "I'm floating on air," he said.

His mother squeezed his hand. "That's the pill, you silly."

By the time he said goodbye to her, though, and they pushed him into the operating room and lifted him onto the cold metal table, all his drowsiness had left him. "I don't think the pill's working anymore," he said, but nobody answered. Was Dr. Pipken even there? A big disk of light on the ceiling beat down like the sun, and like the sun, it hurt Frank's eyes to look directly at it.

He started to pray, squinting against the light. Our Father who art in heaven ...

"Let's get this show on the road." It was Dr. Pipken's voice. Frank tried to sit up but a hand on his chest prevented him.

"Pinky's not here," somebody said.

"Where the hell is she?" Dr. Pipken's voice again.

"I'll go look."

"Goddamn!" The doctor's language was one of the things Frank's mother didn't like. Once, in his office, when she interrupted his train of thought with an ill-timed question, he actually swore at her. Frank would never forget the look on his mother's face. He half expected the police to burst in and arrest the doctor on the spot. When they didn't, Frank's mother stood up to her full height, turned, and walked out, leaving Frank and Dr. Pipken together in awkward silence. "Well," the doctor said at last, "I guess we two guys can talk now." The trouble was, neither of them knew what to say.

Frank couldn't see the doctor from his position on the table, but he could hear him pacing the room. "Where is she?" he shouted.

Frank closed his eyes. Hail, Mary, full of grace ...

"Okay, that's it," Dr. Pipken said. "We're starting."

"But Pinky—"

"Can go to hell."

Holy Mary, mother of God …

Two hands were gently placed on Frank's temples, and a woman's voice said, "Here comes the ether, sweetie. Breathe deeply."

But as soon as he caught a whiff of the cloyingly sweet gas, breathing it was the last thing he wanted to do. It was terrible stuff. Didn't they know that? He wanted to remove the mask to tell them but they had his arms pinned.

He gagged and kicked. "He's a strong one," he heard one of them say. Then all he could hear was the sound of the gas surging through the tubes like a windstorm. He tried to open his eyes, but where the sun had been was only blackness now.

That's when the earth must have cracked and opened. Because he was falling. Below, the catacombs—vast and tortuous, exuding an odor of sweet decay—waited to swallow him.

HE WAS SICK for two days with the ether, vomiting repeatedly, though there was nothing to come up. Sometimes he imagined he could still smell and taste the heavy sweetness of the gas, and this alone was enough to start him gagging. It was as if the anesthetic had settled into the cells of his body or had seeped into some more essential part of him and could not be expelled. Compared to this misery, the throbbing in his feet was a mere discomfort.

He moaned, he wept. "You just go ahead and let it all out," his mother told him.

At least Bucky wasn't around to witness his suffering or to say, I told you so. Before Frank ever regained consciousness, his roommate had packed up and gone home, leaving behind only one thing. "What in the world?" said Frank's mother, opening the drawer of the nightstand. She had discovered the jar that contained Bucky's tonsils and adenoids. Using just two fingers, she dropped the jar into the wastebasket. "Good riddance."

She decided to sleep in Bucky's bed to be near Frank. Two different nuns tried to get her to leave and failed; they promised to report her to their superiors. "I don't care if you report me to the Pope," she told them.

"And you a Catholic," said one of the nuns.

"I'm a mother first."

The next night, too, she faced them down. There were three of them this time, including the head nurse. They were big women and they kept their jaws set and their arms crossed in a way that suggested bodily force was not out of the question. Frank's mother must have anticipated this possibility because she stood up by the side of her son's bed, warning that the first one to touch her would have a lawsuit on her hands. "I just might be suing the hospital anyway," she informed them. She said she had a strong suspicion the anesthesiologist had administered an overdose to Frank.

"You must leave," the head nurse said.

Her answer was to take the sheet from Bucky's bed and wrap it around her shoulders. "You leave. I'm staying with my son." Draped in the white sheet, vigilance issuing from her every pore, she looked like the picture of the guardian angel that hung over Frank's dresser at home. Despite his pain, he could have cried with joy and gratitude that such a creature belonged to him and he to her.

Although the nurses threatened a severe dressing-down by the surgeon in charge, Dr. Pipken was conspicuously absent in the days following the operation. Only his assistants came to check on the patient. Dr. Pipken, they said, was working around the clock on an emergency, putting together the mangled victims of an accident.

"I'll bet," Frank's mother said. She had learned from her son of the doctor's tantrum in the operating room, and she claimed he was too embarrassed to show himself.

But if his mother looked on the doctor's non-attendance as a moral victory, Frank saw it otherwise—as a judgment on him. He worried that Dr. Pipken simply had no use for him after the cowardly way he'd resisted the ether. This concern, even more than his unexpected suffering, threatened to cast gloom over his remaining days in the hospital.

Frank's mother could tell something was wrong. She thought it was the USS Yorktown. "Your father shouldn't have sent it. It's too big and complicated." Frank feared she was right. Each day he sat in his bed with the box open on his lap, trying to decipher the instructions and sort out the parts, but he could not master the thing. When he closed his eyes at night, pieces of gray, molded plastic swirled in his head. When he awoke, there was the big box at the foot of his bed, reproaching him with its full-color picture of the finished vessel. He longed to hold that cunning assemblage in his hands. But doubting he ever would, he felt his longing turn into something else—it became, first, queasiness, then actual revulsion. Sometimes as he studied the parts spread out before him, the unmistakable smell of ether would steal over him and he would reach instinctively for the bedpan.

One afternoon while straightening the room, Frank's mother paused over the scattered pieces of the aircraft carrier. "Darned boat," she said, as if she'd been the one struggling with it all along. She swept the parts into their box like crumbs from a table, then clapped on the lid. Frank pretended to watch a Popeye cartoon. "I think I'll just get this out of our way," she said, removing the box to a chair by the door where her purse was.

She'd picked up a game in the gift shop downstairs. It involved moving marbles around in a circle. If you landed on a space where your opponent's marble happened to be, you could send him all the way back to the start. The game was called Aggravation.

Frank didn't want to play.

"What's wrong, afraid I'll beat you?"

"I just don't want to play, okay?" He'd come to feel as if he were the victim of an injustice. He couldn't name his grievance or say who was to blame, but it had something to do with the ether. He knew that. The ether had ruined everything. Bucky had tried to warn him. He missed Bucky. No new boy had come to take his place. It was just Frank and his mother all day, she having been given time off by Mr. Horgan. The nurses kept their distance.

Frank's father had promised to visit, but the storm in Buckner had torn down his fences and scattered his animals over half the county. He was still rounding them up. Whenever Frank thought of this, he smiled, picturing a scene bigger than life—his father striding across the fields on his mission of retrieval, a cow under one arm, a pig under the other. Frank knew his father would not stop until all the animals were in one barn again.

AT LAST A new roommate appeared. Ronald was about Frank's age but was small and frail and prone to sobbing when there were no adults around to hear him. He was quiet with his tears and must have thought Frank couldn't hear him. But Frank always knew because Ronald's bedsprings squeaked when he cried and occasionally a peculiar gasping sound would escape from the boy, as if somebody had a pillow over his face and was attempting to smother him.

Frank had tried, the first time he was alone with Ronald, to fill the new boy in on hospital life. He spoke of the food, of the nurses, of the rules that might be broken. He even broached the subject of anesthetic and hinted darkly at the existence of catacombs. The briefing was not a success. Ronald just sat there, as pale and brittle as plaster-of-Paris, saying nothing. Shortly thereafter the crying started. Ronald's tears might have filled Frank with scorn. Instead they embarrassed him. Maybe it was an answering catch in his own throat that made him feel implicated in the boy's wretchedness.

Frank's mother drafted Ronald for Aggravation. "This game needs some fresh blood, Ron." She'd played several times with Frank by now, but he hadn't proved much of a rival. "You look like a winner," she told Ronald. But as soon as she landed on a space with one of his marbles, she hooted and said, "Back to square one for you, son."

Frank thought he detected a shimmer of tears in Ronald's eyes, though he knew the boy didn't like to cry when adults were present. "Don't worry, Ronald," he said. "You and I'll get revenge."

"Hey, no fair ganging up," Frank's mother said.

"C'mon, Ronald, we'll get her," Frank said. "We'll murder her."

"Frank, I don't like boys talking that way. We can have fun without that."

But even as she spoke, timid Ronald, in what amounted to a grotesque imitation of slyness, ventured a wink in Frank's direction. Just one tear escaped down his cheek in the process, and it was quickly wiped away.

THAT NIGHT FRANK woke up to find Ronald standing beside his bed. There was no telling how long he'd been there. His unconscious face hung in the darkness as pale and abiding as the moon.

"You okay, Ronald?"

As if this were just the signal the boy had been waiting for, he threw his leg over the side of the bed and crawled in next to Frank, nestling his head in the crook of Frank's arm. "Hey," Frank said, but not so loud as to wake Ronald. Even asleep, this boy felt breakable. Frank considered buzzing the nurse but couldn't reach the button without jostling his roommate and possibly dumping him on the floor—the bed was narrow. So there they were—stuck. "Damn," Frank said. And liking the sound of this, he repeated it to the darkness. "Damn, damn, damn, damn."

Ronald gave a soft groan.

"There, there," said Frank, absently. He was remembering his first night in the hospital. Maybe tomorrow he'd try again to explain some things to Ronald. He wanted to tell the kid about the ether, for one thing. Not to scare him but to get him ready for it. The trouble was, there would be this awkwardness between them in the morning. Ronald would feel embarrassed when he realized where he'd spent the night.

Just don't make a big deal of it, Frank told himself. Say, "Well, old sleepy head, did you have a good snooze?" No, that sounded like somebody's mother. Maybe say, "How's your coperatus seem to graduate?" That was better. Maybe get one of the nurses to dig the clodhoppers out of the closet—if his mother hadn't already thrown them away. Show the clodhoppers to Ronald, with their big bubble toes and laces all the way up the ankle, like something Lil' Abner would wear, or a clown in the circus.

Then Ronald would start to relax a little. Then he would see, everybody has something to be ashamed of.

DECEPTION

My mother said she felt sorry for him because he was new in town and all alone. But Art Campos didn't look to me like any object of pity, arriving for Sunday dinner in that black Impala with the convertible top and fins so long you'd swear the thing was meant for ocean travel. True, he limped slightly coming up my grandfather's front walk (wounded in Korea, my mother said) but appeared light enough on his feet in spite of that.

My grandfather wanted to know how he was settling in. "Oh, swell," he said, stretching his long legs in front of him and crossing them at the ankles. "I love the countryside." We lived in the suburbs, twenty minutes from downtown Kansas City—hardly the countryside. But to Art it must have seemed like the wide-open spaces. He told us his ancestors made their living from the land, back in the old country. "Maybe I'm a farmer at heart."

"No, you're not," said my mother, who knew a little about farmers from having lived with my father. "Art is from Chicago," she reminded us. He'd transferred into the same office where she worked as a secretary. He was in sales.

"If you feel like getting your hands dirty sometime," my grandfather told him, "I keep some chickens in a vacant lot down the block."

"It's a hobby of his," my mother explained.

"Got a rooster?" Art asked.

"No," my grandfather said, "they're just laying hens. I'm the only rooster around here, I guess."

My mother excused herself to check on things in the kitchen, and when she came back she said dinner was ready, we should go into the dining room. She looked flushed and happy making this announcement. She wore her pink cashmere sweater from church and a gray woolen skirt with a petticoat underneath that made the skirt flare out, emphasizing the thinness of her waist and ankles.

"Papa," she said to my grandfather, "would you please ask the blessing?" We crossed ourselves before and after the prayer, and so did Art, which made things friendly all around. When we lived with my father he would sit stiff and silent through grace, staring off at some invisible horizon, as if expecting the Pope himself to come riding up in his gold carriage.

Art said he hadn't sat down to a meal this good since leaving Chicago. It reminded him of the buffets he used to go to down near the old stockyards. "Only nicer," he said, looking at my mother.

"I remember those buffets," she said. "The men where I worked used to take us there for lunch." My mother had lived in Chicago for a year, after the war. The Windy City was one of the things she and Art had in common.

He mentioned the name of a restaurant. My mother turned to me. "Frank, you've never seen so much food as they had at this place. Tables and tables. Heaped up! Too much food really." Her eyes fluttered, her voice dropped. "You felt it was wrong somehow. All that food, with hungry people out begging on corners. I never saw beggars on the street until I lived in Chicago."

Art pursed his lips and shook his head, as if he would have spared my mother this particular experience of his hometown. "You can find the whole world in a city that size," he said. "Good and bad." Did we know there were more Polacks in Chicago than in Warsaw? More colored than in the Congo?

"We've got enough of those two kinds in this town, thank you," my grandfather said.

"Papa, hush. Art will think you're prejudiced."

"Heck, no," Art said. "It's just table talk."

"People are different in a big city," my mother observed. "The girls I knew in Chicago, for instance, they were certainly different." Something in her tone—or maybe the color in her cheeks—caught my attention. We all must have looked at her strangely.

"Well, it's true, you know it is," she said, appealing to Art. "The girls I worked with, at least, they were … faster. And so coarse sometimes. My jaw would drop. The things they'd say … and do …" Her voice trailed off in a way that made me lean forward in my chair.

Art said my mother was absolutely right about the girls in his hometown. "It's the cold wind off the lake that gets them acting that way. Makes them frisky, you know." He shot me a wink.

"Now you're teasing," she said, but didn't seem to mind if he was.

HE EVENTUALLY RENTED a little house only a couple blocks from us, so we saw him often. Sometimes after work he'd appear at the door still wearing his tie, the sleeves of his white shirt rolled up, his coat in one hand and a six-pack of beer in the other. "Everett!" he'd call out. That was my grandfather's name. "Everett! Let's go tend to the livestock!" Then they'd saunter over to what Art called the "chicken ranch," sit in lawn chairs under the lean-to my grandfather had built for his hens, and "watch the sun set." My mother wouldn't let me go along. It wasn't just the drinking; she believed all chickens to be carriers of disease. "If you bring lice into this house," she warned them, "I'll have you both soaking in a tub of disinfectant." But she didn't really object to their visiting the chickens. When Art, in response to her threat about disinfectant, flapped his arms and clucked like a hen in distress, she laughed just like I did.

On the afternoons he wasn't with my grandfather, he often played catch with me. He was a lefty. "A southpaw from the South Side," he said. Or so the papers had described him when he pitched for Loyola University. "That's before the Army drafted me and I got this bum knee," he said, with a hint of bitterness at what fate had done to him. Occasionally he would entertain me by throwing his curve. Unless he signaled ahead of time by holding the ball in front of him and cocking his wrist, I could never tell when it was coming, because he used the same delivery and nearly the same speed as with his fast ball. Art said that was the whole point with the curve: "The batter thinks he's getting one thing but he gets another."

At age eleven I had the feeling everybody could see right through me—my friends, my teacher, especially my mother. I wanted that power to deceive. "I'm going to be a pitcher," I told Art. "Teach me the curve."

"In a few years maybe. You could ruin your arm."

The danger involved made me want to throw it all the more. Finally he relented, taught me what he called the "nickel curve"—a curve ball with training wheels. We propped a piece of plywood against my grandfather's garage for a backstop, and Art would stand there, bat in hand, impersonating a baffled hitter while I fired away from the makeshift mound we'd constructed with dirt from my mother's garden.

It didn't occur to me to question how or why he'd become such a part of our lives, but my mother seemed anxious to explain the situation. "Art and I are friends," she told me once.

"He doesn't have a family of his own," I noted.

"He did have. He had a wife."

"Where is she?"

"She ran off. Back in Chicago. Before Art came here."

"Ran off?" From Art? I pictured one of those crazed dogs you see running loose, dragging a piece of chain or a torn leash behind it. Not knowing what's good for it.

"They're divorced," she said.

"You and Dad aren't divorced."

"No, the Church doesn't believe in divorce."

"But you don't live together."

"I've explained that before. Your father is happy on the farm and we're happy here at your granddad's."

"Uh-huh. Is Art your boyfriend?"

"He's not. That's why I wanted to have this talk. So you'd understand. I'm married to your father. And in the eyes of the Church, Art is still married to his wife, too. That's why he and I could only be friends. Just like you and he are friends."

"Does Art know that?"

"He knows I want to be his friend and nothing more."

"He has dates with other women."

"Yes, he does." A certain tightness had crept into her voice. She knew a couple of the women he dated from the office and didn't approve of them. I had the idea they were like those girls my mother had known in Chicago, the ones that made her jaw drop. "Art needs to meet a nice girl," I heard her tell my grandfather, "like Luray." But her younger sister, my Aunt Ray, lived in California, so I didn't see how that would do Art any good.

According to Art, he wasn't ready to be "serious" about anyone. Besides, knowing my mother had spoiled him for other women. He let this slip once when we were all playing pinochle around the dining room table. My mother folded her cards. "If you're going to talk like that, you can just go home," she said. "I mean it." It was hard to tell whether she was more angry or embarrassed. "Now, Patsy, take it easy," Art said. My grandfather and I smiled at each other, like the whole thing was a joke, which maybe it was. Imagine kicking Art out of the house.

It was true he'd been kicked out of the Church though. "Cut off from God's holy family" was how my mother put it. In other words, excommunicated because of his divorce. "But it wasn't even his fault," I protested.

"Life isn't always fair," she reminded me, with a sad, far-away look.

ART OCCASIONALLY WENT back to Chicago to visit, and he talked of my going with him sometime. We could catch a ball game, he said, take a boat ride on the lake. He said Lake Michigan was no different from the ocean: stand on the shore and look out, all you could see was water, and more water. But my mother said no way I was missing school to go off galli-vanting. I didn't complain much. In truth I felt a little relieved by her opposition to our travel plans. I guess I shared some of her apprehensions about that cavernous city where bums roamed the streets. She always said she was glad for the year she spent in Chicago; it had opened her eyes to the world. Still, she'd never been happier to return home.

Art brought me back a pair of athletic socks from Chicago once. They were knee-highs, made to resemble part of the uni-form of the White Sox. But the best was yet to come, he said. He had a brand-new baseball at his house, but we weren't going to play catch with it. He was keeping the ball in a drawer so it wouldn't get scuffed or dirty, and the next time he went home he was going to have it autographed for me by some of his buddies on the White Sox. He mentioned Luis Aparicio and Nellie Fox by name. "Only the best double-play combination in baseball," I explained to my mother.

"You don't say." She seemed suspicious of Art's gifts. He'd brought her something, too. "What in the world?" she said, when she opened the box. "Pants!" She held them up.

"They're called toreador pants," he said.

"Because when you put them on," my grandfather said, "all the young bulls come running after you."

"The sales girl told me they can't keep them in stock," Art said. "All the ladies are wearing them."

"Ladies?" my mother said. I'd never seen her in pants.

Art said, "I thought if anyone had the shape for them …"

She wouldn't try them on for him but later modeled them for my grandfather and me. "They don't leave much to the imagination," my grandfather said. The pants were black and tapered and close-fitting. I never paid much attention to my mother's shape, didn't often think of her as having one. She did though, and the pants made it impossible not to notice. I tried whistling but it only came out as air, like a teakettle before it boils.

"Honestly, if Art thinks he can turn me into one of his women—" She acted put out, but stood looking at herself in the mirror anyway, turning sideways, tracing with her cupped palm the long, smooth curve of her hip.

I NEVER MET any of Art's "women," as my mother called them, except once. My mother had agreed to let him take us to The Pit, a well-known barbecue spot in the colored part of town. "You come, too, Papa," she said. But my grandfather declined: "I don't go down there and I don't expect them to come out here."

"That's the past talking," she said.

"Like the man in Washington keeps telling us," Art said, "it's a New Frontier."

"That's right," said my mother, who'd stuffed envelopes for Kennedy.

But my grandfather wouldn't budge. On the way to the restaurant, my mother asked Art, "Do you really think it's safe?"

"Sure, I've been there plenty of times. Besides, it's the best barbecue anywhere."

The Pit was the only place I'd ever been, except professional ball games, where blacks and whites rubbed elbows. The customers were crowded together around Formica tables, tearing meat from bone, sopping up sauce and grease with slices of bread, and washing it down with frosted mugs of beer. Art waved at a goateed black man in a red apron whose job it was to hook the slabs of beef and pork and turn them on the grill. The man saluted us with the long, curved tongs he used for the meat. Over in one corner, a woman's laugh, sudden and shrill, caused us all to stare. The woman was white, the man she was sitting with black. Art shrugged. "This is a place to let your hair down." My mother smiled uncomfortably, a glaze of perspiration clinging to her brow. "Take your coat off," he said, but she shook her head. She was wearing the toreador pants and must have felt embarrassed about showing them off in public. Especially here, where people regarded one another with frank, appraising looks, hailed each other in loud voices.

Halfway through our dinner, a red-haired woman in a white fur coat came and stood over our table with her legs apart and her hands on her hips. (Later my mother would say, "Imagine wearing a fur to eat barbecue!") The woman said to Art, "I thought if you were going to ignore me, I'd just come and say hi myself."

"Why, Sharon." Art pushed back his chair, started to get up, then didn't. "Sharon Kinney."

"He remembers me, after all," she said over her shoulder to a plump man in a gray suit who stood behind her. She had a boisterous, teasing way about her, and was very pretty. I noticed some people at other tables looking at us.

Art introduced Sharon to my mother and me. "Sharon's a friend of Carol from work," he said to my mother.

"Carol?"

"Carol in filing," Art said. "You know."

My mother smiled vaguely. Even I could see she had no idea who Carol was. Sharon Kinney cocked her head. "Carol," she prompted. "Carol Waymer. Frizzy, black hair? Flat chest?"

My mother gazed up at Sharon with the same sweet, uncomprehending expression on her face. Sharon turned to the plump man standing behind her. "Carol knows her all right." Then she added something I didn't quite catch, something about "airs." The plump man gave a little snorting laugh.

"Cut it out, Sharon," Art said in a tone I'd never heard him use before. The smile that had been on her face vanished at once.

"C'mon, Sharon," the man behind her said. "We were just on our way out, remember?"

"Sure, sure, in a minute." She stared down at Art, who would not meet her eyes. She opened her purse and reached inside. A gun! I thought. She seemed like the kind of woman who might do something like that. Instead she removed a pack of cigarettes. She put one of the cigarettes between her lips, then bent toward Art, weaving a little as she waited for him to light it. That's when she appeared to notice me for the first time, though Art had already introduced us. "Hi, sweetie. What's your name?" The unlighted cigarette wagged on her red lips.

"Frank," I said.

"Frank. That's a nice old-fashioned name. Hi, Frank."

I felt my mother's hand on my knee.

Art produced a flame from his lighter and offered it to her. His hand was trembling slightly. She put her own hand on his, to steady it, and accepted the light. "There," she said, straightening up and exhaling. "No reason for anybody to get on their high horse. We're all friends here. Isn't that right, Frank?" My mother squeezed my knee and I knew to keep my mouth shut. Then, as abruptly as she'd appeared, Sharon Kinney turned from us with a flourish of her white coat, followed closely by the plump man in the gray suit whose name she hadn't mentioned.

Art kept apologizing on the way home for taking us to that place.

"I really don't know any Carol in filing," my mother said. "I hardly ever go down there. Mr. Horgan says he won't have his secretaries running their legs off between floors. That's what the office boys are for."

"Was that lady—the one who knew Art—drunk?" I asked.

"Isn't it a shame?" my mother said. "Such an attractive girl, too."

Art looked at her across the front seat. I was sitting between them. "You're worth a dozen of her," he said, his voice thick with emotion.

She kept her eyes forward. "Art, watch up ahead—that truck, it's turning!"

He flicked the wheel of the Impala to give the truck a wide berth. As he swerved, we were all pressed momentarily together. "Golly," she said, "that's the last thing we need, to have an accident in this part of town."

SHORTLY AFTER CHRISTMAS, my grandfather went to visit Aunt Ray in California. It always made my mother nervous to be left alone. She feared burglars. Knowing this, my grandfather arranged with Art to keep an eye on us while he was gone. But that didn't seem to relieve my mother's anxiety. In fact the precautions she took against intruders were more elaborate than usual. Not only did we push large pieces of furniture in front of all the outside doors before going to bed—standard procedure when my grandfather went away—but we booby-trapped the windows as well, placing my old toys on the sashes so they would clatter to the floor and wake us if anyone tried to get in. In the past I'd played my part in these preparations enthusiastically; it was fun to be scared. This time I was old enough to resent being implicated in my mother's hysteria. I reminded her Art lived only two minutes away: "All we have to do is pick up the phone, he'll be here in a flash."

"We can't always depend on Art," she said.

Since when? I wondered. It was true, though, we hadn't seen him much lately. He'd spent Christmas in Chicago. I remembered the presents he'd brought us from there once before and also the autographed baseball he'd promised. Our Christmas tree was still up, and I was hoping the ball with the signatures of Fox and Aparicio would appear under it any day. My anticipations, then, ran to matters other than intruders. Nevertheless, my mother did her best to get me into the spirit of the occasion. Together we pulled the mattress from my bed into her room. "It'll be like camping out," she said. Since I'd never actually been camping, the comparison seemed plausible enough to me. "Only instead of wild animals," I said, beginning to like the idea, "it's robbers we've got to watch out for." I got my "flame-tempered" Louisville Slugger from my room and lay on the mattress, the bat at my side.

Not long after we were settled the phone began to ring. "Never mind," my mother said when I started to get up. The phone was in the kitchen, and since we'd moved a chest of drawers in front of her bedroom door I probably couldn't have gotten to it in time anyway. "Maybe it's Granddad calling to see if we're all right," I said. "Or Art. It might be Art."

"I can't help who it is," she said. Then she added, "I'll call your granddad tomorrow so he won't worry."

"And you'll see Art at work."

"That's right."

Still, I couldn't help thinking it was a flaw in our burglar system that the phone was unreachable. It rang on and off for the next hour. "I'm going to move the dresser," I said at last.

"Leave it," she said sternly.

"I can't sleep," I complained. "Every time I close my eyes, the ringing starts."

"I know it, sweetie. I'm sorry. If we just stay put, he'll give up in a minute."

"He will? Who?"

"I don't know. Whoever's calling. Look, let's say the rosary to take our minds off it." She handed me the beads from her night stand and began to lead us in the Sorrowful Mysteries. Together, we prayed for the virtues of resignation, mortification, humility, patience, and love of our enemies. What came to me instead was drowsiness, forgetfulness, and finally sleep.

All the next day in school the talk was of a big storm blowing in from the plains. By the time the bus dropped me off that afternoon, the flakes had started to fall. "It's snowing!" I announced, bursting through the front door. My mother was sitting at the dining room table and I could see she'd been crying.

There were flowers everywhere—red, yellow, blue—on the tables and chairs, in the corners, in the middle of the floor. It was snowing outside, but it looked like spring in here. My first thought was that somebody had died. "Is Granddad all right?"

She nodded. "Everybody's fine." Except her, she wasn't fine. "What am I going to do with them all?" She handed me two pots of red ones. "Here, dump them in the trash outside."

"But where are they from? Who sent them?"

"Never mind. I want them out of here. Wait a minute." She went into the kitchen and brought back some of the brown paper sacks she saved from her visits to the grocery store. We put all the flowers in the bags, then I carried them outside one at a time and stacked them by the trash cans in the back yard. When I was finished, there were over twenty bags piled up. It made me a little sad, all that color hidden away, destined for the city dump.

By nightfall the snow had covered everything, and the bags of flowers out by the trash resembled a huge, slumbering polar bear. My mother heated some soup and we watched TV. When it was time for bed, we re-enacted the precautions of the night before. I said I didn't think any burglars would come around on a night like this. "You never know," she said.

I lay on the mattress beside her bed, fiddling with my transistor radio. I was looking for WLS, "the voice of Chicagoland," which Art had introduced me to. But tonight the storm muffled the signals of even the local stations. "Why don't you turn that off and come up here with me?" she said. "You haven't gotten so big that you don't want to cuddle with your mother anymore, have you?" I said, no, I hadn't, and I crawled in next to her. "You don't need that thing," she said, taking the Louisville Slugger and dropping it on the floor.

Her bed was the same one she'd slept in since she was a girl. It was soft and sagged in the middle, and the middle was where you always ended up. Just before I fell asleep, I heard her voice, as soft and thrilling as a lullaby: "You know what this storm means? No school or work for us tomorrow."

I WOKE IN the dark. My mother wasn't in the bed. "Go away!" I heard her saying. "Go on!" Her voice was coming from over by the window. "Get out of here!" It sounded as if she were attempting to discourage an unruly pet—a large dog perhaps. Not a burglar. "Frank's here. Frank's here in the room with me," she said. "You'll wake him up!" These last words she uttered in a fierce whisper. Somehow I took this as my cue, clambering out of the mushy bed, stumbling over the mattress that lay on the floor, and bumping into my mother. She screamed.

"Hey!" came a man's voice from outside. "You all right in there?"

"It's Art!" I said, relieved.

"Frank?" he said through the window. The blinds were drawn, I couldn't see him. "You oughta be asleep by now."

I started to open the blinds, but my mother slapped my hand. "We're just fine in here," she said to the window. "We *were* asleep until you came along."

"Go to the front door," I told him, "we'll let you in."

"Frank!" she said. "You hush!"

Already I was pushing aside the chest of drawers that blocked our way. My mother squeezed through the crack in the door ahead of me. "You stay here," she said. There was a knock at the front door. "I mean it!" But as soon as she turned to go to the door, I was right behind her.

"C'mon, Patsy, open up," Art called.

"No."

"Ah, baby, please. I thought we understood each other. I thought we had something."

She looked at me, her eyes wild. "I think he's been drinking," she hissed. "What are we going to do?"

I began to be a little alarmed myself. My mother resembled a crazy woman standing there at the door in her bare feet, her hair falling down in her eyes. Her gown was askew; a muddy-brown nipple winked at me through one of the gaps between buttons.

"I'm getting my bat," I said.

When I came back from the bedroom, I could hear them talking to each other through the door. "I told you it's impossible," she said to him. "Now, please, Art, you're scaring me."

"I've got a key," he said teasingly. "Wait a minute. Somewhere here. Yup, here it is."

"Art!" she said.

"Everett gave me it. Perfectly legal. The Church won't mind."

"Art, remember, Frank's here!"

"Frank, you still up?" he said, in an injured tone. "You should go to bed, Frank. Your mom and I got some adult things—"

"I've got a baseball bat," I warned.

"That's nice. Can't play right now."

"Art, think what you're doing," my mother pleaded.

"Oh, shit," he said. "Wait a minute. Key fell in the snow. Now where the hell—"

"Art?"

"Ah, c'mon, Patsy. Whaddayafraidof? Open up."

"No."

"Let me in, goddamnit!" He started pounding on the door. Then it was quiet. "Please," he said. "We could talk."

I crept to the window and peeked through the blinds. Everything was white outside, all the usual landmarks obliterated.

"Can you see anything? Is he leaving?" she asked.

I shook my head. "I'll bet it's cold out there."

"Whose side are you on anyway?"

"What do you mean?"

"I mean Granddad's not here. I need you to be strong for me."

"Okay."

"Come here, you talk to him. He might listen to you." She whispered to me what I should say.

"I don't want to."

"You want me to call the police to take him away? Because I don't know what else to do. If he starts yelling again, he's going to wake the neighborhood! C'mon, try. For me."

So I addressed myself reluctantly to the front door: "Art, it's Frank. Can't you please go home now? You're making us afraid in here." My mother prodded me. "I'm scared, Art, and Mom's real upset. I think she may be calling the police right now."

"She'd better not!" he yelled. "The crazy— Listen to me, Frank. I don't know what she told you, but I'll bet it's not the truth. She led me on. Boy, did she!" He didn't sound like himself; his voice had become almost a whine. "She fooled me good. You tell her I'm going now. But you tell her the girls at work were right about her. Miss High-and-Mighty! Miss Holier-than-Thou! I'm going now, but you tell her. Tell her where I come from they got a name for someone like her!" Then a strange word exploded at us through the door; my mother encircled my head with her arms, as if to shield me from it. "You hear that, Patsy?" Art yelled. Then he repeated it just to make sure.

We kept still and waited. After what seemed a long time, she said, "I think he's gone. Let's go back to bed, it's freezing." We lay huddled together with the light on.

"I don't get it," I said after a while. "Aren't you and Art friends anymore?"

I felt her shiver. "I'm afraid Art turned out to be, well, not the sort of man I thought he was."

"Is it because he's divorced?"

"That's part of it, I guess. People want different things sometimes, that's all. They end up disappointing each other. They don't mean to."

I thought of the flowers in paper bags lying outside under the snow. "Art disappointed you?"

"Yes, he did."

"And you disappointed him?"

She sighed. "I guess I did. I'll tell you one thing, I'm sorry it happened. I'm sorry the whole thing happened."

She wasn't sorry for Art though. "What's a cock teaser?" I asked. Her whole body stiffened and her face went hard. "Barnyard talk," she said. "We don't use words like that."

By the time my grandfather returned from California, the snow had melted and our Christmas tree had been carted off with the trash. It was plain winter now, without any of the window dressing. In those days, the sun rarely climbed above the roof tops; it struck trees and houses at blunt angles, submitting every object to its withering glare. "I hate this time of year," my mother said. "Everything's so ugly."

I agreed with her about the season but had a plan to cheer my own heart. One day I set out for Art's house, walking with my shoulders hunched up and my hands in my pockets, my ball glove dangling from my wrist. I'd told my mother I was going to the church to play on the blacktop. She objected that it was too cold for baseball. I said it was never too cold. She pointed out I didn't have a ball. Somebody would have a ball, I said. Somebody always did. Especially after Christmas.

She used to say she could look at me and tell when I was lying. She was right, too. I could always feel the muscles around my mouth contracting into a queer, embarrassed smile whenever I tried to fudge the truth with her. Not this time though. This time I kept my face as composed as the saints in church, as self-possessed as the athletes' faces on bubble gum cards.

"All right, go ahead," she said. "But I think it's sort of odd to be playing baseball in the winter."

"Spring training begins for the major leagues in just two weeks," I said, marveling at my own glibness.

Art's Impala was in his driveway; it needed a wash. According to Art, the salt they used on the roads would eat the paint off a car in no time. He believed in taking care of a vehicle, in treating it right, then it would treat you right. The Impala, he said, was the most responsive car ever made. It had push buttons on its dash and an ivory knob attached to the steering wheel, and sometimes he would lean back in the seat with just one finger on the knob and steer that way. "This is what they mean by fingertip control," he said. But he wouldn't do it with my mother in the car.

People liked Art. My mother remarked on that. It was a valuable trait in a salesman, she said—likability. It was something you couldn't teach, and Art had it. She didn't love him though. I knew that because we hadn't seen him at our house in more than three weeks and she didn't seem to mind a bit. Sometimes after the dinner dishes were cleared and my mother and grandfather were playing pinochle or gin rummy and I was finishing my homework in anticipation of some TV program, she would glance up from her cards, look at my grandfather, then at me. "Isn't this nice?" she'd say.

I wondered what it was Art lacked, which prevented her from missing him. I wondered it as I stood on his front stoop, reading the initials in the aluminum scroll on the screen door: TDB. Not his initials. Probably they belonged to the family who lived here before, the ones Art was only renting from. I thought of Art's wife running loose in Chicago. Of Art himself cut adrift from the Church, and now us.

"Life isn't always fair," my mother said. But sometimes there were valuable consolation prizes. I rang the bell, looking up at the cyclops eye on the door with the same guileless expression I'd already practiced on my mother. "Merry Christmas," I said, when he opened up. "Happy New Year." As if nothing had passed between us except these two holidays.

"Hey, Frank. Same to you." He looked over my head toward the street, perhaps checking to see if someone had brought me. He was in a blue flannel robe, though it was after lunch on a Saturday.

"Want to play some catch?" I said.

"Your mother know you're here?"

"Not exactly. Want to play?"

"Better not," he said. "Knee's sort of acting up." He pulled back the flap on his robe and turned his leg so I could see the scar. "Damned V.A. doctors never fixed it right," he said. "Never trust doctors, Frank. That goes double for government doctors."

It was clear he felt himself to be the victim of an injustice. "You should write to President Kennedy," I said.

"You sound like your mother. St. Jack'll fix everything! Listen, Frank, Mr. Kennedy's not half the man she believes he is." He smiled to himself in a way that wasn't a smile. "No man is."

"At least, Kennedy's trying to help people," I said, defending my mother's hero.

"I guess I'll help myself," he said. It sounded like he was dismissing me, but I hadn't forgotten what I came for. I lingered on the stoop, staring into the upturned palm of the glove I'd slipped on my hand before ringing the doorbell. From the empty mitt I plucked an invisible sphere and gripped it the way he'd shown me last fall, index and middle fingers pressed together along what would have been the top seam, thumb braced underneath, so my hand formed a half-circle.

The pantomime was not lost on him. "If you're going to practice the curve, you better have the ball," he said.

"You mean the one you got me in Chicago?"

"The very same."

"The one you've been saving?"

"Uh-huh."

"With the autographs of Nellie Fox and Luis Aparicio?" I studied his face.

"Sure. Absolutely. Wait here." He withdrew into the house.

"Sorry it took a while," he said when he returned. "I forgot where it was for a minute."

I turned the ball over in my hands, scrutinizing the signatures. Anyone could see they were forged. That's what took him so long. The thing was, he hadn't even made the two autographs look all that different.

"You don't want to play with that ball," he said. "You want to save it. It's worth something."

"Okay," I said, putting the ball in my glove and backing off the stoop. "See you, Art."

"See you, Frank. Oh, Frank!" I was already at the driveway. I stopped and turned around. "Those guys—Luis and Nellie," he said. "They said tell you, hi. Hi from Chicago."

I smiled and waved, feeling like an idiot for letting him think he'd tricked me.

On the way back to the house, I kept spitting on the ball and rubbing it in my hands until the fake signatures were smudged beyond recognition and the horsehide cover resembled one large bruise. I went into the back yard and hurled it several times at close range against the plywood backstop we'd put up last fall. After the horsehide was good and scuffed, I remembered what Art said once about a nicked ball being a pitcher's best friend because it jumps around more on its way to the plate and no batter can touch it. So I tried a few curves, but to my eye they all appeared perfectly straight. Then I was really mad at the ball, because obviously it had no curves in it. I got one of my grandfather's screwdrivers from the toolshed and jabbed at the seams until they loosened and I could peel the cover off.

Inside, the ball was nothing but tightly wrapped string. It took me an hour at least to unravel it. I held the end of the string and heaved it against the sky, watching the ball get smaller and smaller, until something black, about the size of a marble, separated itself, fell in a graceful arc, like a tiny meteor, struck the tin roof of the toolshed, and bounced into a corner of my mother's garden. This I retrieved, holding it up to the sun, rolling it back and forth in the palm of my hand, examining the thing for many minutes—this unsuspected core, as weightless as a robin's egg, as impervious as rock—which seemed, after all, the answer to some riddle.

FROM THE
BLEACHERS

We'd hated them casually for years. Maybe if we'd been more diligent, more concentrated in our dislike of them, they wouldn't have taken over like they did. Now they were impossible to ignore. They leered at us from around corners or giggled when we walked by. They tapped their feet on the backs of our desks, and when we turned around to see what they wanted, they'd pull a face, as if to say, what are you looking at.

I wore a crew cut and so became a special target of theirs. "Love the hair! Whose little boy are you?" When one of them asked if she could run her hand over it, just to see what it felt like, I sheepishly submitted, tipping my fuzzy dome for her to pet, feeling the prickles from her fingertips all the way down my back. "Oooh, gross," she said when she was finished. "I'll have to wash now. I'll bet you've got lice. I'll bet that's why your mama cuts your hair short." I might have hit her, but somehow—when had it happened?—she was beyond my reach. I might have said something—something fatally cutting. But what? Such wanton cruelty as theirs rendered us mute. We didn't know what to say.

We kept an eye on them. Sometimes at recess a group of us would gather on the old concrete bleachers in left field and watch them playing kickball. They were hopeless at kickball; that much hadn't changed. Whether kicking or throwing, everything they did looked unintentional. They played as if in a dream, their minds not on the game. We smirked at each other.

The concrete bleachers made giant stair steps in the outfield. In a few years the coaches would have us bounding up and down them like goats, but for now we sat cross-legged or lay on our sides. The bleachers were ancient and cracked. From their fissures grew weeds and tufts of grass and these we worried with sticks and sharp rocks, sometimes forgetting the enemy and lapsing into a reverie of excavation. We were great diggers, our hands rarely empty or idle. Then some recent outrage would snap us out of it. It was reported, for example, that one of them had phoned one of us.

"Oh, man!"

"What *for?*"

"If one of them called me, I'd tell her—"

"Eat it!"

"Yeah."

"They are so—"

"Creepy."

"They stink."

"Pheewwwy!"

So, one of them had phoned one of us. What did it mean? In a way this development was more unsettling than their previous disdain. Apparently they needed us, had an urge to make contact. Where might it end? Still, we knew what it was to be needed. Our parents needed us, helplessly sometimes. Now, it seemed, the enemy did, too. Perhaps it was our fate to be needed. In a way it put them in their place, revealed a weakness, we thought.

Sitting in the bleachers, we experimented with all sorts of names for them, pronouncing the words like incantations, as if to cast out spirits. But none of the names quite did the trick. Until one boy who had older brothers said in a high voice, "You know what they are?" There was a look of transport on his red, sweaty face. We stopped our digging, quit fidgeting altogether. "Bitches," he said. Our prophet. "They're dirty bitches, is what they are." We held our breath, letting the word sink in. It was an odd, religious instant.

The teacher strode to a spot in between the kickball diamond and the bleachers. She put a whistle to her lips, thrust out her chest, and blew. Recess was over. The girls fell in behind her, leaving their halfhearted game without a backward glance. They stood in line looking up toward the bleachers at us, their arms crossed, their hips jutting out. Everything about them said, what are you waiting for?

A STATE

OF

DISREPAIR

W hen Sky went to stay with her parents for the summer, Louis followed uninvited a few days later. His idea was to patch up the relationship, but soon after he arrived he bought a sports car and spent much of his time with it. He often dreamed about the car. It would take him spinning along the Gulf, sometimes putting up sails and skimming the waves. Once it even sprouted wings and soared with Louis into a pink tropical heaven.

His girl friend occasionally came along in the dreams. As it turned out, things weren't as bad between Louis and Sky as he'd feared. Friends back home had expressed alarm over her plans to spend the summer apart from him, and Louis had eventually caught their concern. Now he thought he'd been silly to listen to them. True, she'd seemed a little distant when he appeared at her parents' house, but in the midst of her close-knit and eccentric family she always seemed distant. Sky and her parents were a mystery to Louis. With their bright clothes, their alert eyes, and their short, tufted haircuts, they were like exotic birds ready to take flight should he blunder too near. They were cordial enough on this visit, however, and sometimes, late at night or early in the morning, Sky went beyond cordiality. Between his girlfriend and his car, Louis didn't regret making the trip.

Though the car was old, it appeared to be in perfect condition. Its most recent owner had been a well-to-do elderly man. His widow showed Louis to the garage where the car was kept under a cover. "He was so tender toward this automobile," the old woman said, "that he could scarcely bring himself to take it out on the road." She viewed cars as mere transportation. Not this one though. "I think it scorns having to run along the ground."

Louis had heard such cars could be temperamental. But when he turned the key, it started at once. The old woman clapped her hands. "You must be right for each other." Louis saw his reflection multiplied in the many crystals of the instrument panel. He was grinning extravagantly.

He took Sky and her parents for rides. But since they weren't car enthusiasts, their appreciation left something to be desired. Louis enjoyed himself more when he rode alone, and his girlfriend and her parents seemed content with this arrangement. When he wasn't driving the car, he was cleaning and polishing it, or running some errand for it.

One day he met a man who knew all about the car. Louis had gone to a shopping center to buy a special treatment for his convertible top. The man was sitting in a battered orange station wagon. "Nice car," he said, as Louis was walking past. "You keep it in good condition."

Louis explained he'd just bought the car, it was the previous owner who'd kept it in good condition.

"I know," the man said. He named the old gentleman whose wife had sold Louis the car. "I used to work on it for him."

"Oh, did it need much work?" Louis didn't really want to know. The repair history of any vehicle made a sordid story, and he would have preferred to imagine his car was an exception.

The mechanic didn't go into particulars. "They're beautiful cars—but funny." He was holding a sleeping baby along his forearm and in the palm of his hand, as if it were a violin he meant to play. As a matter of fact, Louis thought, he looks more like a musician than a mechanic. He had a thin, dark face and black hair that was swept back like a conductor's.

Louis asked if cars like his were supposed to run hot in the summer.

"They're cold-blooded. If yours is running hot, there's something wrong with it."

Louis felt a sickening thrill in his stomach, as if he'd just gotten word he had a serious illness. He couldn't say he was surprised.

The man with the sleeping baby told Louis not to worry. He gave him a soiled card with a phone number and a map on it. The place where he worked was twenty miles away in a town Louis had never heard of. "Wayside is the armpit of Texas," the man said. "But it's a good place for the repair business. They come to me in Wayside from all over."

By now the man's wife had appeared with more children in tow. Her husband handed her the sleeping baby with one hand as he flicked the ignition switch with the other. Louis noted the confident surge of the engine. He watched the wagon go. It had a bumper sticker on the back—a cactus, like a twisted cross, emblazoned by a purple sunset. The sticker said, "We've Been to Paradise Valley."

When Louis called Wayside the next morning, he was told that Stefan, the man from the parking lot, didn't come in until nine o'clock.

"What kind of mechanic doesn't go to work until nine o'clock?" Sky wanted to know.

Louis picked at his breakfast, wondering the same thing. Sky's father thought it odd that Louis intended to drive to Wayside. Once it had been something to see, he said, a beautiful place, with an artists' colony. But that was years ago. "The bay receded and left them with nothing but puddles."

Louis said he wasn't going to Wayside to look at the scenery but to get his car fixed.

"Of course," said Sky's father. "It's just that I'm used to thinking of Wayside as a place where things break down, not get fixed."

"Last year a freeze killed all their palm trees," Sky's mother said. "All you see there now are naked stalks sticking out of the ground. It's a shambles."

"You'd expect them to cut the dead trees down," said Sky's father. "In Wayside, they just wait for them to fall over on things." He seemed to recall a newspaper story about a Wayside man who was killed by a falling palm tree while sitting in his car at the Dairy Queen.

Louis pushed his chair back from the table. "Don't worry, I'll watch out for falling palm trees."

Sky said, "I hope you don't think you're funny."

THERE WERE VERY few palm trees to watch out for in Wayside, and little of anything else. The apparent exception was trains. Not that Louis actually saw any trains, but he did cross a surprising number of tracks. It was as if a large and intricate iron net had been cast down on the place, though for what purpose was unclear since Louis detected no other signs of industry. So much empty track—obviously well-maintained—in such an empty landscape made him feel as if he were overlooking something important. He went slowly and watched carefully at the crossings, conjuring out of the silent, heavy air sudden locomotives to pulverize him.

When he got to the shop, Stefan was on his knees in front of an engine. The engine rested on a bench that was dangerously bowed, and Stefan was trying to prop up the bench. Louis had never seen an unhoused engine before. Its height and the dark, gnarled mass of its nether portions surprised him. He thought of the charred stump his father and some other men had once pulled out of the front yard at home. Clinging to the roots had been clots of mud with live, tangled things in them.

Stefan left his engine to examine Louis's temperature gauge. "It shows hot, all right," he said. He opened the hood and pulled the spark plugs. "See there? Your fuel mixture in the front carburetor is too rich."

"Is that why it's overheating?"

"Most problems aren't this or that. Everything in these cars is connected."

"Uh-oh."

"That's the wrong attitude," the mechanic said. "First you look and try to understand."

Louis watched as Stefan tested the pressure in the cooling system with a device that, when placed over the mouth of the radiator, produced a sound like breathing. Next the mechanic drained the cooling system and disconnected the hose that led from the radiator to the engine. From inside the hose, which still contained some of the blue-green coolant, he plucked a tiny silver object the shape of a fish. He held it in the palm of his hand for Louis to see. "The thermostat," he said. "It looks fine."

"That's good," Louis said.

"Not necessarily. Something's causing your car to run hot. I've already checked the easiest and cheapest things to fix, and they're okay. Now we're getting into the expensive stuff."

While Stefan was under the car, another customer drove up in a sports model that was older and perhaps even better preserved than Louis's. The husky, bearded man who got out was smiling and shaking his head. "Dang thing died three times on the way here." He placed two small boxes and a plastic sack at the feet of Stefan, who had not come out from under the car. "Got some presents for you, Stefan."

"So, Eugene, your parts finally came in?" Stefan still didn't come out.

Eugene pulled up his belt and glanced around the shop. "See

you had to take that poor fool's motor out." He seemed a little embarrassed to have his packages lying on the floor ignored.

"Your car?" he asked Louis. "Pretty nice."

"Thanks."

"You got my condolences."

"What?"

"Come here."

Louis followed Eugene over to his car.

"Nice," Louis said.

"Mint. Absolutely mint." Eugene pointed to a place on the trunk lid. "Except for this." There was a single chip in the paint.

"I don't think anyone would notice it."

"Doesn't matter whether they do or not. With cars like yours and mine, you worry all the time."

"I'm not a big worrier."

"I don't mean just about paint chips. A car like this gives you big things to worry about. Look at all the instruments. Hell, I'd rather try to read a female's moods. One damned gauge or another is always acting strange. What's wrong with yours?"

"Temperature gauge."

"See what I mean?"

Eugene said he'd come to have his carburetors rebuilt. "But that's not so bad. Come around here, I want to show you something." He took a large cellophane package from behind the passenger seat and handed it to Louis. The bundle of wires inside was blue and red and pink and contained different sizes, all entwined like so many veins, arteries, and capillaries.

Louis handed it back. "What is it anyway?"

"A wiring harness. Not even Stefan'll fool with the wiring on these cars."

Stefan was out from under Louis's car. "The water pump looks okay."

"You're lucky," said Eugene.

Stefan winked at Louis. "Eugene thinks these cars are possessed."

"I wouldn't be surprised," Eugene said. "Look at who you have to get to work on the things. A Greek—in South Texas—working on a British sports car! Right there you start to wonder."

Stefan shrugged.

"Tell me, does he even look like a mechanic? What is that you got on, Stefan, a tunic? And what kind of mechanic wears sandals? He's not a mechanic, he's a goddamned guru."

Stefan raised the hood of Eugene's car, and the big man fell silent. As the mechanic peered in at the engine from one side, Eugene peered in from the other. Stefan grasped one of the carburetors with both hands and twisted it sharply in its socket. Eugene straightened abruptly. "But what the hell, they're great cars. Some of my best times have been spent in this car. I remember when my wife and I finally got it all fixed up. We had three new coats of lacquer on it and ten coats of wax. One day we took off down the coast. Just sailing along in this great-looking car, all the people waving at us. Sometimes we'd stop so my wife could photograph the birds. Even the birds were cooperating that day. We got pictures of birds we'd never seen before. Of course, on the way back, in the middle of nowhere, the car broke down. They towed us to the nearest place—here. That's how I met Stefan.

"You think I regret anything about that day? Absolutely not. Not even breaking down. A car like this teaches you not to take anything for granted.

"Hey, what's that for, Stefan?"

The mechanic had a mallet poised over the engine. He gave the motor a smart whack with it, then another.

"I can't watch this," Eugene said. "Let's go get something to eat."

Louis walked with Eugene toward a cluster of buildings that wavered in the heat about a half mile down the road. "My wife is the mechanical one," Eugene said. "When I met her she had the parts of a Peugeot scattered all over her garage floor. It looked like there'd been a damned explosion or something. I said, 'Girl, it looks like you got some mechanical difficulties.' She said, 'Nothing a miracle couldn't fix.' She wasn't a bit worried."

"She ever get it back together?"

"A guy finally came and carted it away in boxes. She's pretty mechanical though. She'd have enjoyed watching Stefan with the carburetors."

"Why didn't you bring her?"

"We're not together anymore. She sort of took off."

Eugene said he knew of a barbecue place. "Great burnt ends." Louis didn't know what burnt ends were, but it didn't matter. When they got there, they found the place had closed down. "Nothing makes it here for long," said Eugene.

"Stefan seems to do all right."

"My car alone would keep Stefan in business. Besides," Eugene added, "he doesn't require much. You know he delivered their last kid himself?"

"Really? I saw the baby."

"Looked healthy enough, I'll bet. Stefan usually knows what he's doing. He's got this thing about self-sufficiency. He thinks civilization's going bust and we're going to have to fend for ourselves."

"I'm surprised." Louis would have thought Stefan too level-headed to harbor survivalist notions.

"I don't know," Eugene said, "every time I come to Wayside, I feel a little like the world was going to end myself."

They walked to the Dairy Queen. Louis had a giant Dream Float, but Eugene, who had lost his appetite in the heat, simply had a Seven-Up.

Eugene said he didn't feel bad about the money he put into his car. It all came from royalty checks, and he'd always looked upon the checks as grace money. Several years ago he'd composed some music for marching bands, and the checks just kept coming. For ten years Eugene had directed a high school marching band. Band directors, he claimed, were like football coaches—the good ones shared the same thrill of seeing all the different parts come together in a well-drilled unit. But it had become too easy for Eugene to whip marching bands into shape. He felt like a fraud doing it. "I want a music store. I find out today if I get the loan." He said there was no reason why he shouldn't. "But who knows how banks work?"

It occurred to Louis they must be sitting in the same Dairy Queen where the man had been crushed to death by the palm tree. The story Sky's father had told struck him as even more implausible now than this morning. He mentioned it to Eugene.

"It really happened," Eugene said. "I knew the guy. He was sitting right out there in his car eating a Peanut Buster Parfait." Eugene took Louis outside and showed him the exact spot.

"But there's not a palm tree in sight."

"Sure, not now."

They stopped at a small grocery store on the way back. Eugene wanted to buy a jug of water for Stefan. The cooler in the shop was broken, he said. "Do you think he knew I was kidding about the way he dresses?"

"I think so."

"It's hard to tell with Stefan. All the time I been coming out here, I'm still not sure he likes me."

"He doesn't let on much, that's true," Louis said. "Here, let me pay for part of that water."

"Sure, we'll make it a joint offering."

When they returned, they found Stefan probing under the hood of Louis's car. The shop had darkened because a locomotive had appeared on the track outside and was blocking the light from the garage door.

"When did that come?" Louis asked.

"I don't know," Stefan said. "They come through here all the time."

He said he'd adjusted the carburetors and the timing. "It's running cooler, but it's still too hot. There's something not right down in there, but I can't see what it is. I think it's safe to drive."

"Are you sure?" Louis asked.

"One thing worries me. There's a danger you might have cracked the cylinder head."

Eugene gave a long, soft whistle.

"If you did, that would explain why we're still getting the high temperature reading."

Stefan removed the cover from the cylinder head and began searching with a wand-shaped light for the spills of oil that would indicate a cracked head. It seemed to Louis as he watched the light move over the engine that a new and forbidding landscape was being revealed to him, one he would rather not know. Why had he let himself in for this aggravation by getting such a car in the first place? Because he'd been enamored of its lines, that's why. Because it was beautiful—almost a work of art. But that wasn't all. He'd been drawn, too, by the power and complexity of inner workings he didn't begin to understand. Now he saw his ignorance might have serious consequences. Maybe he wasn't clever enough to own such a car. Maybe you had to know as much as Stefan. And if that were so, how would you ever have time for anything else?

Stefan said the head wasn't cracked.

"You're very lucky," said Eugene, sounding slightly let down.

Louis wondered. Was it luck? Or was there a measure of tolerance, a margin for error, in these affairs after all?

"I guess I'll be off then," he said. Life was forgiving.

THREE DAYS LATER Louis spotted Eugene at the beach. The big man was sitting on the sea wall, staring out at the water. He didn't seem to notice the seagulls hovering above him. They were holding themselves so still they seemed to be suspended from invisible wires.

"I didn't get the bank loan," Eugene said. He wasn't giving up his plan to buy a music shop though. "I'm taking the necessary measures." For one thing he was going to start saving the money he got from his music.

"I thought that was for your car," Louis said.

Eugene held out his hand. There was a stir overhead, a sudden crowding down of wings. In his palm was a brilliant piece of chrome, a winged woman in a flimsy-looking robe, which Louis recognized as the ornament from the front of Eugene's car.

"You sold it!"

"Yup. But Stefan let me keep this. He doesn't care much about hood ornaments."

Louis felt sorry for Eugene, losing both the loan and the car. He looked beat. "Think of it this way," Louis said. "Without the car, you won't have so much to worry about."

But Eugene wasn't after consolation. "I did the right thing getting rid of it," he said.

Eugene had other news. His wife had called him out of the blue and she was interested in the music shop from a business angle. They were going to talk about a partnership.

"That's great," said Louis. "Sounds like you two'll be getting back together."

"I hope so. You never can tell. I've been sitting here trying to figure out what went wrong the last time."

Louis couldn't get over running into Eugene again. He motioned to Sky to come over, but she was some distance away and didn't see him. When he looked for her again, she was dashing into the surf.

WAKE UP!

I ask her, "Is everything off downstairs?"

"I think so."

"Yes or no?"

"I'm pretty sure."

"The gas?"

"Almost positive." She's not a bit concerned. Never mind we could end up asphyxiated in our bed. So I go down to check. Everything is off. And by the time I crawl in next to her—no more than two minutes later—she's already asleep, as if to prove what an effortless thing it is to lose consciousness.

I haven't slept in three weeks, though she claims that's impossible. "You've slept, you just don't remember it." Maybe she's right. But if I have no memory of waking up, does the sleep do me any good?

I turn on my side, studying her. In profile her face has the serenity of a mountain range, with her turned-up nose the highest peak. And here am I, stranded on the barren plains.

She was not always so indifferent to my plight. When this ordeal first began—did I say three weeks ago? it's been longer, I'm sure—she plied me with back rubs, warm baths, hot toddies, and prescription drugs. We talked into the early hours about what might be troubling me and spoke of getting professional help. She tried gamely to interest me in lovemaking; it would relax me, she said, take me out of myself. But sex is the last thing on an insomniac's mind.

Finally she gave up, went back to sleep. "After all," she said, "it won't do for both of us to be exhausted. Then where would we be?"

She's a good sleeper, my wife. It's hereditary. Her mother and father, brothers, sisters, cousins, nieces and nephews, all are prolific dozers and nap-takers. You should see the family gatherings, check out the scene at her parents' place after a holiday feast. They're sprawled on couches and in chairs, on the floor, heads flung back, mouths agape. So many insensate bodies, in such attitudes of rapt slumber! You wouldn't expect to find anything like it outside a nursery, or an opium den.

I burrow my elbow into her ribs, she moans softly and rolls over, giving me her back.

I do my deep-breathing exercises, say my prayers. Later I go into the bathroom, fill the sink with warm water, and plunge my wrists in to soak them. My hands float palms up, looking pale and defeated in the bright light.

Back in the bedroom, I stand over my sleeping wife, bending down so my face nearly touches hers. It seems to me at such moments that sleep—what separates me from her—is but a thin membrane, like the film that floats on still water, and I should be able to penetrate it. So I press my face close to hers and bore a single thought into her head—wake up! But she's not paying attention; her eyes roll around in their sockets, rippling the papery lids as she scans her dreams. Where is she? And who is she with? Sometimes I poke and prod her, seeking to dislodge some clue from her subconsciousness, and sure enough, now and then, a name finds its way to her lips. "Carla." Or "James." Also: "Scooter, Daddy, O.J., Mrs. Nuchols, Sandra Day O'Connor, Lois," and somebody called "Tito." I marvel at what a well-attended affair my wife's sleep appears to be; and yes, it hurts my feelings a little that my own name has yet to turn up on her guest list.

Once I worked my hand under her nightgown, took the soft flesh of her hip between my thumb and forefinger, and pinched—hard. She sat up and stared at me blindly, not all there. "Who's this Tito?" I demanded. She smiled—a girlish, inscrutable smile—and sank back down among her pillows.

Downstairs I drink a glass of water, swallow a pill, then flip on the tube. The caption on the screen says "Live Dance Party." The dancers are mostly teens who seem galvanized by the idea they're breaking rules—staying up all night! Their frenetic good humor and self-conscious naughtiness is almost enough to put me to sleep. For a second my mind is transported to an open field, where, in the middle distance, blackbirds have alighted on the bare branches of a solitary tree. It occurs to me the birds are starlings, like the ones that used to visit my parents' farm in winter. What's more, I'm asleep! But like the wizard's name that must not be uttered, sleep vanishes—the birds scatter like buckshot—and I'm left staring at the tube, where some black girl is taunting viewers, thrusting her large ass at the camera again and again.

I trudge upstairs, making a lot of noise on the way. I pee in the bowl without closing the door, flush the toilet—twice, then throw myself down on the bed with enough force that one of the wooden slats holding up the box springs clatters to the floor. She doesn't bat an eye, my sleeping beauty, though a kiss might wake her. I feel somehow it would.

I yank one of the pillows from under her head, put it over her face, and press down, just to see what will happen. She's been so inert up to now it surprises me how full of fight she is all of a sudden—writhing and bucking, flailing away with her fists—as if on some level she's been expecting this and is ready for me. I fall back before her onslaught, curling into a ball and wrapping the pillow around my head for protection. "Stop it," I plead with her through the layers of down and feathers. But the knee she drives into my kidney serves notice that the long period of her forbearance is at an end. "It was a stupid joke," I protest. "I'm sorry, I didn't mean to scare you. Can't we forget it? Can't you go back to sleep? Can't you, please, just go back to sleep?"

VIGIL

Sometimes she believed the professor was devoted to books only and superior to all else. There was a cartoon on his office door that showed a solitary whale in an easy chair, smoking a pipe and wearing little eyeglasses, reading. Rosita supposed it was a cartoon; the humor escaped her. To her, the professor was unfathomable, like one of those grand and rarely glimpsed creatures that travel under the sea, harboring thoughts and feelings, possessing a whole secret language she would never know.

Still she thought she detected loneliness in his long, pale face and in the days and nights he spent by himself in his office. It was part of her job to empty his wastebasket and dust his bookshelves, and sometimes late at night she would let herself into his office with the pass key and there she would find him bent over his books. "Pardon," she would say, feigning surprise. She had seen the light under his door. "No problem. Come in, come in," he would say, removing his glasses and seeming actually pleased to see her, though probably he would have been grateful for any human presence at that deserted hour.

The languid smile with which he greeted her on these evenings reminded Rosita for all the world of her own small son emerging from a deep slumber. As with her son, she wanted to cradle his head against her, offer him what tenderness there was in this life. Perhaps he wouldn't have minded, who knows? She was pretty. Everybody said so, even her sour friend, Esmerelda, and her uncle's *gringa* widow—Rosita's aunt—who disapproved of her.

But in spite of her looks she did not know how to touch him. She knew that prettiness, though it gave her hope, was not enough. Nor were the purity and unselfishness of her intentions enough. For this man of books she would need words, and she did not have the words.

Then one night she found them—many words—in the professor's wastebasket, of all places. Not his words but those of another. Rescuing the floral-embossed and scented pages from the trash and hiding them in her pocket, she knew they were love letters even before Esmerelda's reading of them confirmed it. Not even the mocking tone in which her friend recited the words diminished Rosita's pleasure in hearing so many of her own private feelings for him poured out in those lovely pages. Then Esmerelda mentioned the obvious: "He throws her pretty letter in the trash. How important can it be to him?"

Could it be even words were not enough to touch him? "She is his student," Rosita said. "Such a thing from a student, it is beneath him."

But if a student was beneath him, what about her? "Don't worry, *hermosita*," said Esmerelda, who did not miss much. "Men like to go beneath themselves. It's more pleasure for them that way."

Esmerelda had a way of looking always on the disagreeable side of things. Not for the first time in their brief acquaintance, Rosita wished circumstances had provided her with a more sympathetic companion. But then very little had turned out as she hoped since coming to the North.

She expected too much, according to her aunt, who had arranged for the papers to bring her here. Having grown up without advantages herself, her aunt said she once believed it impossible for the poor to be spoiled but that she'd changed her mind since knowing Rosita's family. "Your mother's brother, my husband, before we had a dime, went for a shoeshine every day and a haircut weekly. 'Let me cut your hair,' I said. But it wouldn't do for anyone but a barber to touch that head of his. Your mother, bless her, had the same great vanity. It led her to expect too much from life. Lord save us from beauty!"

Rosita had to hide a smirk whenever her aunt spoke like this, for clearly the old woman's prayer had been answered in her own case. The family had always wondered what trick this dog-faced *gringuita* had used to get such a handsome husband.

Rosita's aunt wanted her married and off her hands. She had in mind as a suitor the man who cut the grass for her and did odd jobs. The man's truck, which Rosita had consented to ride in once or twice, said "Fixit" in hand-painted letters on the side, and everyone called him the fixit man. He was nearly as old as the aunt herself, and Rosita disliked most things about him, but especially his hands, with the crooked fingers and horny, yellow nails.

"That old woman thinks she can force me to marry," Rosita complained to Esmerelda, "all because she pays the rent for my falling down apartment." It was Esmerelda who'd first informed Rosita that her aunt had settled her in a part of the city inhabited increasingly by blacks. On the subject of the fixit man, however, Rosita's friend took the aunt's side. Esmerelda had never met the fixit man, but she read all the newspapers in the supermarket and claimed to know human nature. "Take my word, there are many worse men. Besides, do you want to live in the *Proyecto del Mar* forever?" Rosita did not. She hated "the Project," as her black neighbors referred to the place. The name made her think of something ill-planned and haphazard, permanently unfinished.

ROSITA NEVER WORE her uniform on the long bus trip out to the university. She wore heels and slacks, sometimes a dress. It flattered her to imagine the other passengers taking her for a student, a secretary, or better yet, simply an attractive woman on her way to meet someone. She carried her uniform in a shopping bag.

Once at work, she changed clothes in the maids' utility closet but even then would not concede entirely to the routine and drudgery of the job as represented by the aquamarine skirt and blouse she was required to wear. She would tuck a handkerchief in her breast pocket or tie a colorful scarf in her hair, perhaps even pin to her blouse, above her name, a marigold filched from her aunt's yard or a geranium from one of the planters that lined the university's walkways. She adored flowers, would spy whole patches of them growing wild along the road and wish she were not riding the bus so she could stop and pick them. She'd heard it was against the law in this place to help yourself to the wild flowers, and while this made no sense to her, she accepted it as true. Still it might be worth the risk. Some star grass for her hair would be lovely, she thought.

In whatever way she adorned herself, she did so with the idea the professor might somehow notice and approve. He had become a constant, largely invisible presence in her life, and she frequently consulted his imagined likes and dislikes. She hoped it wasn't a sacrilege, but she believed she had even begun to pray to the professor, though this had not been her intention at first.

It happened because sleep was difficult for her in the Project. Always there was the pungent odor of strange foods. And always there was noise, especially from overhead, where the man who lived directly above her spent much of the night hammering and sawing. Whatever he was building, Rosita thought, it must soon be completed. But it never was. It helped her at such times to picture God the Father standing over her bed in the dark, smiling down on her and sweetly speaking her name—"Rosita, Rosita, Rosita"—until she lost consciousness. Lately though, when she asked God to protect her, it was in the professor's voice that He answered, whispering her name in the darkness, in a tone so loving that she did not worry about her black neighbors or her loneliness or anything. Such episodes sometimes approached the miraculous and Rosita would feel herself to be actually embraced by the professor and at the same time filled with his spirit.

She had so much she wanted to say to him. Failing that, she poured herself out to her son, Rudy. Such a bright boy, he watched her with solemn, dark eyes that seemed to understand or at least to catch the drift of her words. He was the easiest child to have around, so quiet and good Rosita would forget him at times, losing herself in some reverie. Then coming to her senses, she would go through the apartment in search of her baby and, finding him, would hug him and lavish kisses on him. For a small child, he had little patience with maternal affection and would start to squirm. "Oh, that's all right, run away," she once blurted out, her eyes filling with tears. Perhaps there was something wrong with her, she thought, something that frightened people away or drove them off.

Even Rudy's father, a fisherman from her village whose sturdy handsomeness had given him substance in her eyes, had proved ultimately elusive, drowning at sea before they could be married. They had made love just once, and then only at his insistence. It happened down by the water, along the deserted February shore, and all Rosita remembered of it, even the next day, was the hard sand against her buttocks, the pounding of the waves, and the fact that she could not breathe. Perhaps this was why her sadness over his loss was tempered with relief, in spite of the discovery later that she was pregnant.

She did not believe it was right for her son to grow up without knowledge of the fisherman, so she made it a point to talk to him about his father. The trouble was, the man she had been going to marry no longer occupied much of a place in her memory. Perhaps because he had drowned and his body was never recovered, she could only visualize him as if through a watery film, in which he looked vague, half-formed, like pictures she had seen of unborn babies. By contrast, the professor was always vividly present to her. So when she talked to Rudy about his "papa," she began to endow the fisherman with qualities she had observed in the professor. First she gave him long, expressive hands and a wistful expression; she gave him gentle manners and eyes the color of blue sage. Then she gave him an absorption in books and a subsequent need for glasses to correct his nearsightedness. She marked, too, a carelessness in how he wore his tie (she wanted to straighten it) and in the way he had of getting chalk dust on the back of his coat (he must have leaned against the blackboard as he taught, and she always felt the urge to dust him off, and once, without thinking, she had. So she had touched him!).

"Your papa loves us and watches over us," she assured her son. And as always Rudy seemed really to be listening, taking into his heart everything she could think to say about the rare fisherman who was his father.

ONE NIGHT ROSITA observed a girl slip something behind the cartoon on the professor's door. The Scotch-taped clipping served as a pocket for her delivery. The girl walked away quickly, with her head down, passing right by Rosita, who was sitting at a study carrel at the end of the hall. She was pretty and well-dressed, this girl, not scruffy like some of the other students. Rosita was certain she had been crying as she hurried past.

After waiting to make sure the student would not come back, Rosita went down to his door (no light shone underneath), removed the envelope embossed with flowers and scented with perfume, held it briefly to her breast, then put it back.

The next night when she came to clean his office, the letter was lying wadded up in the trash. "Ay!" Rosita felt the pain of those crumpled words in her own heart. What could this strange man want that he should treat with such contempt one who loved him? He lives only in his books, she told herself. The truth of this could be seen in the shelves that lined every wall of his office and were so high she had to climb a ladder to reach them. What chance against this mass of books had a few scribbled words? No more chance than flowers cast on the sea. And what chance had she who could not even scribble the few words?

She sought out Esmerelda and found her leaning against her cleaning cart by the elevator, reading a newspaper. It was their usual spot for unscheduled breaks, because if a supervisor came along they could pretend to be on their way to another floor.

"River Yields Killer Cupid's Latest Victim," Esmerelda read with a reverence grisly stories inspired in her. She held the newspaper up in Rosita's face. Under the headline was the shadowy picture of a woman's naked corpse. Rosita averted her eyes but not before glimpsing a large hole in the dead woman's chest.

"Put it away, Esmerelda. It will give me bad dreams."

"All right, look, it's gone. You bring out the devil in me, you know it?"

Rosita wondered at her friend's appetite for gruesome things and believed Esmerelda's outlook might improve if only she lost weight and paid some attention to her appearance. A cheerful nickname would help, too, for Rosita had a strong faith in the power of names to influence disposition. This was how she explained her own love of flowers. But once when she had proposed "Essie" as a substitute for "Esmerelda," her friend had spoken harshly to her: "If you're so perfect, why don't you learn to read and write English then?" Now Rosita was more careful about what she said.

"I found another letter," she told Esmerelda.

"He doesn't show his love bird much respect, does he?" said her friend, taking the crumpled pages from her.

"What could be wrong?"

Esmerelda's eyes scanned the letter. "The love bird has changed her song."

"Read it, Esmerelda."

"It will make you blush. The love bird has become the dog in heat. She writes what she would like him to do to her with his male part. She has several uses for it in mind."

"No! Her heart was breaking when I saw her."

"But not for long, she has plans for your professor to make her very happy." Esmerelda read the letter. Such language Rosita could not imagine any woman using with the professor. "She has ruined her chances with him," she said.

"You watch, now she will succeed."

"Esmerelda!"

"I'm serious."

"You said yourself, he throws her letters in the trash."

"But the words sink in here." Esmerelda tapped her head with her finger, smiling slyly.

ROSITA'S AUNT KEPT pressuring her about the fixit man, letting it be known that her financial support could not always be relied upon. Besides, she worried about Rudy, she said. "The poor child doesn't know what it is to have a man around."

"My son," Rosita said, "is very devoted to his father who died."

"Don't be silly," her aunt said. "How could he be? He never even … Don't be silly, Rosita."

"I am not silly, Aunt. I speak all the time to my son about his father."

"You're a silly girl. That boy needs a real father, one who's alive."

"I tell my son everything about his poor father," Rosita said. "I tell him what a fine man he was, how lonely he must be without us, how we will all someday be together. My little one loves to hear it. His papa is alive to him. He is alive to both of us, even though we do not see him."

One day Rosita's aunt met her and Rudy at the door of her house but did not invite them in. She had had enough, she said. Really, at her age, she had no intention of assuming any permanent responsibility for her dead husband's relations from Mexico. She had tried to do a good turn, but people who possessed neither gratitude nor common sense could hardly expect infinite patience from others. It had all been very upsetting to her, she said. On and on the old woman went, like an ugly little dog yapping at an unwanted visitor, and when she finished she sagged against the doorframe and started to cry, throaty and dry-eyed. Her tearless sobbing seemed to Rosita the last despicable resort of a woman without heart.

That night Rosita dreamed she was being chased through the twisting streets of her village. She had taken something that did not belong to her. She could not run fast because she was hindered by the burden of her theft, which she carried in her apron. It felt as if she were carrying bricks, but when they caught her and she let go of her apron, dozens of wild flowers fell to the ground. A crowd surrounded her. "Surely, anyone has a right to pick them," she said, but without conviction. "The whole family's like that," came an old woman's voice. "Not a penny to their name, but nothing's too good for them."

When she woke up, Rosita remembered all the things her aunt had said to her. "Father in heaven, what now?" From her neighbor's apartment upstairs came the sound of hammering. She cowered in her bed, as if from the blows. This was how it felt to be abandoned, cut adrift in a place where it was criminal to pick the flowers but a neighbor might bang away through the night; where pure love must remain silent but a student was free to write filth to her professor. Where your own uncle's wife might disown you. Rosita wished they would just put an end to her, like the woman whose picture she had seen in Esmerelda's newspaper. Then at least her fate would be known. The professor himself would surely learn of it, see the picture and read the words. Possibly it would break his heart.

"You think it's enough to be pretty and to want pretty things," her aunt had said. "Life isn't for those who shrink from it. You have to roll up your sleeves, make what you can."

She thinks I am a fool, Rosita thought, but she is the one fooled if she thinks I will ever let her boss my life again. Her aunt had treated her like the poor relation in every respect. "I can get along better without such help," she told herself, and hoped it was true.

She might have gone back to Mexico except for the professor. He was the sun around which her days revolved. She followed his comings and goings, watching for the light beneath his door, feeling desolate on those days when he failed to appear. What did he do away from the university? What was his life like? She looked up his address and walked by his home one morning. There were no signs of life in his house, which looked like every other. She tried to picture him inside, in his bed sleeping or in his kitchen eating cereal. But these ordinary activities seemed to have nothing to do with him, and she realized that he did not exist for her apart from the university. She could always find him there in her imagination, behind his office door, just as she could find Jesus in church, waiting, quiet and alone within the tabernacle, for someone to love him.

Sometimes as she busied herself in his office, he at his desk, so close, she felt almost faint. This gave her an idea—she might pretend to faint. He would come to her aid. There would be touching. Who knew what might happen? But then she dismissed the idea as a common trick, unworthy of her feelings for him. Besides, she was afraid.

She was afraid most of the time, and of everything. She was afraid of English, though she knew she must learn it if she was ever to become more than a cleaning woman, if she was ever to speak to the professor in the way she wanted. Her aunt had said you have to roll up your sleeves. Rosita had no use for that old woman, but desperation made her willing to try the advice. She borrowed a grammar book from Esmerelda and kept it on her cleaning cart to study in spare moments. She did her best with the book when she sat at the carrel near the professor's office. Then when she began to feel battered by the English words, she could look up from the grammar toward his door, holding fast to the ultimate reward of her labor.

She would now and then place a token on his desk when he was not around, perhaps a chocolate bar or a piece of fruit. Mostly though she left him flowers, especially the bluebonnets and lady's slippers that had begun to spring up in patches all over the university. Did he wonder who left them? Or was he used to receiving anonymous gifts? He must have many who admire him, Rosita thought.

None of her offerings found their way into his trash, and this encouraged her. Perhaps he even guessed who they were from. Yes, he must suspect, she thought. For the love she bore him was so overwhelming it seemed impossible to her it should remain entirely secret and unreciprocated.

ROSITA WORKED FOR three days on the letter, writing her feelings first in Spanish, then translating them as best she could onto the rosebud stationery she had bought in the university bookstore. The finished product looked well enough; in fact, it looked beautiful, for she wrote a lovely hand. But what if the English was wrong? He would think she was stupid and illiterate. The alternatives, however—not to write at all or to ask Esmerelda's help—were intolerable to her. She turned the letter over and over in her hands before finally putting it in the envelope and sealing it. It seemed a promise of something to come, and she liked touching it.

She was so nervous on the day she determined to deliver it that she forgot the shopping bag with her uniform. "I will have to borrow one from Esmerelda." Really she liked being on the bus without the uniform, with only her purse in her lap, the letter inside. It seemed her life was about to change dramatically and forever. Rosita watched her reflection in the window as the shadows of trees and buildings passed over it.

She went straight from the bus stop to his door and slipped the letter behind the cartoon as she had seen the pretty student do. She did not allow herself second thoughts, for fear her nerve would fail. She was still trembling when she met Esmerelda at the maid's closet and asked to borrow one of her uniforms.

"You seem not quite right," her friend said, putting a hand on Rosita's forehead. The spontaneous concern made Rosita think perhaps she had misjudged Esmerelda. She hoped so. She needed someone to be kind to her today.

"My head, you know, it is somewhere else, that's all."

"You're telling me. You forgot to do the second floor last night. Guess who caught hell for it?"

"I'm sorry, Esmerelda. I will do it and the third floor today."

Esmerelda's uniform was too big for Rosita. "Hey, you're not woman enough to wear my clothes," Esmerelda laughed. "You remind me of a little girl playing in her big sister's dress."

"Thank you for the uniform anyway, Esmerelda."

"It's all right. You should take it easy today. Forget about the second floor. One of the others will do it."

It was nice to feel taken care of, to fancy she really was a little girl in a grown-up woman's clothes, pretending to be in love.

At least once an hour she stole a look at his door, to see if he had discovered the letter yet, but it remained where she had left it. She knew he was in the office, she'd seen the light several times. Maybe he no longer reads such letters after receiving that shameless one from the student, she told herself. Or worse, maybe he knows somehow this one is from me. Hers he throws in the trash but at least he reads it; mine he considers not even worthy to open.

"You should go home if you don't feel well," Esmerelda told her later. "You look awful."

"I know," Rosita said, kneading the front of her friend's big uniform.

"What's wrong with you? Does it have something to do with that professor?"

"Oh, look, Essie, what happened to me this morning." She showed her friend a place on her ankle where she had cut herself with a razor. She had been thinking about the professor, not paying attention to what she was doing. The sudden pain had made her cry out.

"It's deep, you will have a scar."

"I don't care." It seemed to Rosita she had wounded herself for him.

"Go home," Esmerelda said. "I'll say you're sick."

Instead of going home she went to the study carrel near his office. Maybe I should take my letter and slip it under the door, she thought. He will not be able to ignore it so easily. But it seemed impossible for her to move, to do more than sit in that place where she had so often kept her vigil. Please, please, she prayed. I will stay here all night if I must. Then she remembered her son, who expected to be picked up at day care. What time was it? Already she was going to be late. It seemed more than she should have to bear, the burden of this love and the duties of a mother, too.

God, I wish I had no child.

No, no, I don't mean it, she added immediately, fearing this one of all her prayers would be answered. She, if anyone, knew how it felt to be forsaken by the one you love. She would never do that to Rudy.

He is all I have.

She hurried to retrieve her letter—it was too painful to leave it there on the door. Her hope of that morning seemed like a cruel trick now. She had her hand on the letter when the door opened.

"Oh, hello," he said. "I didn't hear you there."

She was about to give him the letter, but something stopped her—the sight of another behind him. The pretty student was standing in front of one of his bookcases, running a finger down a row of titles.

"Well, come in," he said to Rosita. "It's all right, I was just opening the door to get some air."

"I love this one," said the student, taking a book from the shelf. "But you've written all over the margins! Isn't that against the law or something for professors?" She held the book open for Rosita to see. "Isn't that bad?"

"It's a paperback book," the professor said, "a tool of the trade." He'd taken up a silver letter opener from his desk and was jabbing at an envelope.

The late afternoon sun was streaming in the window, and the office was stuffy and faintly sour smelling. The professor's tie was loosened and his sleeves were rolled up. His usually pale, ascetic face was flushed. He looked like a man who had been exerting himself. Rosita felt as if a great weight were pressing down on her. It was hard to breathe. She wanted to escape from this place but hadn't the power to move.

"Is that for him?" the student asked, pointing to the letter Rosita was holding.

"Here," the professor said, brandishing his letter opener, "I'll take it."

"No, no," the maid gasped, shoving the thing into her pocket. "It is for another."

"I know what she's after." The professor reached for his wastebasket without getting up from his chair. He put the basket down at Rosita's feet. "Not much for you today."

Rosita was not looking at the trash. She was staring at the pretty student, who showed no trace of the sadness Rosita had seen in her before. With the sun on her golden hair and the teasing expression she wore when she looked at the professor, she appeared radiantly happy.

"Do you two know each other?" the professor asked. "Stephanie, this is—" He glanced at Rosita's nametag. "Esmerelda."

"Oh." Rosita felt the stab in her chest.

"*Esmerelda*, that's a pretty name," Stephanie said.

"For a pretty girl," the professor said.

"Watch yourself with him," Stephanie advised Rosita, but in the teasing way she intended for the professor. "He likes the pretty ones."

Rosita made for the door. "Wait a minute," the professor said. "Don't forget what you came after." In the hall, he pressed the wastebasket into her hands. He was breathing hard, as if he had run a long way to catch her.

THE DISTANCE

FROM

HERE TO THERE

T urning into the driveway, which wound a quarter mile through tall, dense pines back to her house, Eileen had the feeling, magnified, as in a dream, of being late for something and having no good excuse. She'd dawdled in town, unable to decide what to get for dinner, and now darkness was beginning to settle among the trees. Another ten minutes and she might not have noticed the deer at all—a fawn, judging from its size—nestled in the pine needles some distance off the driveway.

She wondered if it was hurt. Otherwise, why hadn't it run off at the car's approach? Or at least stood up? She pulled around the back of the house and parked beside Richard's station wagon, which had not been there when she left. Her husband worked as a defense consultant in Washington but often flew home to Georgia on weekends. Since their son, Adam, had gone away to college, Richard had been coming more regularly, bringing work with him. Eileen understood he was making a sacrifice to be with her.

Their two black Labradors came up to meet her, stretching their necks to see into the car. Her husband said it was a mistake to project human feelings onto animals; it was a form of sentimentality, also egotism. Even so, Eileen knew at times such as these the dogs missed her son and were looking for him. "Sorry, girls," she said. "I didn't bring him with me. We'll see him Christmas though." In the meantime, the animals seemed happy just to be with her, bending their bodies double from the sheer pleasure of greeting, nosing her feet and legs to see where she'd been keeping herself all afternoon.

"C'mon," she said, patting her leg and breaking into a trot that led them up the back stairs and onto the screened-in porch. It was lucky they hadn't discovered the deer yet. "You stay here," she told them, and they sat down side by side. "Good girls." They were called Santa and Diabla, sisters from the same litter, and they were never apart. Eileen envied their closeness and used to say that if one of them died the other would have to be put to sleep, it would grieve so. Richard rolled his eyes at this, perhaps thinking how much the dogs cost. He'd bought them to be her protectors during those times when both he and their son would be away and she would be a woman alone out in the woods. But as guard dogs Santa and Diabla were of doubtful value. "You got me lovers, not fighters," Eileen liked to point out to her husband, a former army officer.

As she was unloading the car, he came around the corner of the guesthouse, walking gingerly, barefooted, along the gravel path, wet trunks clinging to his thighs, water running off his legs. Beads of water were trapped like tiny pearls in the matted hair of his chest, and she had an unaccustomed impulse to touch him there, set the pearls free. Instead she presented a dry, powdered cheek for him to kiss. "How far'd you swim?"

"Seven miles." He smelled of whiskey and chlorine. Typically, he permitted himself one drink on the plane ride home. Like the laps he swam in the pool behind the guesthouse, the drink, she supposed, was part of his weekend letting go, a sort of cleansing ritual. Not that Richard was one of those bureaucrats who required absolution for his sins. On the contrary, he was the most principled man she knew.

"I promised myself I'd keep going until I heard your car on the drive," he told her, still out of breath from his workout. "Any longer and you might have drowned me."

"There's a deer in the front yard," she said, as if this accounted for her lateness. "A fawn. It might be hurt."

"What makes you think so?"

"It can't move, I drove right past it."

His knowing smile irritated her. "That's what they do, Eileen. They hold still. It's their way of not being seen by predators."

"I think this one's hurt. Isn't there anyone we can call to come see about it?"

"It's almost seven o'clock. Who are we going to call?"

A chorus of crickets started up in the trees behind them, as if to announce the night. There were bobcats in these woods. Oh, why had she taken so long in town? "I'll bet it's gone," he said. "I'll bet if you look now it's not even there."

He sounded so sure of himself she almost doubted she'd seen the deer in the first place. But a few minutes later when she walked out to the edge of the forest and peered in, the animal was still there, its silhouette just visible in the mounting darkness. She resisted the temptation to go closer, not wanting to scare the creature. It was so small! Hardly more than a baby. Where was the mother anyway?

Back in the house, she looked for her husband. She wanted him to know that she'd been right after all, that she was not over-reacting. Trouble, she felt like telling him, is not always something we borrow. "Richard," she called, "the fawn's still there." But she received no reply. He kept an office out in the guest house and was probably trying to get in some work before dinner.

Dinner. She'd meant to warn him about that. Tell him not to dress for it. Despite all her deliberations in town, she'd finally settled on take-out. Barbecue. He liked barbecue. Still, she felt guilty, knowing he ate in restaurants frequently and looked forward to home-cooked meals on the weekend. "An army marches on its stomach." How often had she and the other service wives repeated this saying among themselves? Food mattered to their men, and beyond mere sustenance. She herself lived on little more than yogurt, cereal, and coffee during the week. Since their son's departure, it seemed silly to cook only for herself. Richard had remarked, "You're getting as slim as a college girl." She corrected him: "No, as a high-school girl." She and their son's friend, Jessica, who was sixteen, had recently compared the slenderness of their wrists and ankles. "I hope I look as good as you," the girl said, and was diplomatic enough not to add "when I'm your age."

Eileen worried what Adam would say about the weight she'd lost. She did not want him to think she was pining away for him, even if it was true; she did not want to be one of those mothers who hobbled her son. She wondered if this weren't Richard's concern as well, if it didn't explain the cordial distance he always maintained from Adam, as if he were standing back and observing the boy, withholding final approval until he could determine whether Eileen had spoiled him or not.

Her husband had to knock on the screen door because she'd latched it to prevent the dogs from pushing out. "I meant to tell you not to dress," she said. "We're only having ribs from the Wagon Wheel."

"Ribs are good." He'd put on slacks and a starched white shirt, open at the neck. His hair, which was slicked back, looked almost black under the shaded porch light. He leaned down to pet Santa and Diabla, who received this attention with demurely lowered heads. The dogs were so different around him, Eileen noted, as if they knew he was a man and they were ladies.

"Did you get your work done?" she asked.

"Mmm."

Silly of her to ask; his work, she knew by now, was never done. She told him about the deer: "It must be very badly hurt. It doesn't move at all. I think it's waiting to die."

"There's nothing we can do until morning," he said.

She knew he was right, but that didn't make her feel any better.

"I guess it could have been hit by a car out on the highway," he said.

"Or shot."

"Hunters don't shoot fawns, Eileen."

As if all men with rifles behaved according to his rules! This property was posted but that didn't keep the hunters away. She heard gunfire often enough to worry about the dogs' safety and to keep them shut up on Saturdays and Sundays during the season. Sometimes men in camouflage, with guns hitched over their shoulders, would come to the front door requesting permission to hunt; they acted as if they had a right to be there, and often seemed quite surprised when she refused them. She always did say no, firmly but politely, trying not to let them see how much pleasure it gave her. She liked to think of this property as a refuge for the wildlife and had even arranged to have salt licks put out to attract more deer. So the thought of this fawn lying, perhaps wounded, in her front yard filled her with indignation.

"Guess who was here when I pulled in?" Richard said, probably trying to change the subject. "The girlfriend."

"Jessica? You can call her *Jessica*."

"She calls me *sir*."

"You should be used to that."

"Coming from her it makes me feel old."

"Compared to Jessica, we are old."

"I know. It's not *old* I mean exactly. *Out of it.* Maybe that's what I mean."

"All right." Eileen didn't know what else to say. Her husband was hardly the sort to fret over time passing him by. So what was this about? The thought occurred to her, what if he had a woman in Washington, a young thing, who made him age-conscious? She knew so little of his life up there, how he filled up the hours outside work, she supposed it might be so. But probably not. Such conduct would go against not only his religion—Richard was a devout Catholic—but also his character. He was not a man to shrink from loneliness or to welcome personal entanglements. The painting that hung above his desk out in the guesthouse was of a soldier in Confederate butternut leaning against a tree, his forehead swathed in a bloody bandage. Eileen imagined this was the sort of destiny—solitary and honorable—Richard would have chosen for himself. No, she couldn't believe he would have an affair. And yet the possibility of his doing so, the very idea of his being susceptible in such a way, affected her strangely. It was a piquant notion. "You should get Jessica to show you her tattoo," she said. "Then you really would feel out of it."

"Why? What kind of tattoo?"

"A little red heart on the inside of her ankle. The kids do that kind of thing now."

He glanced down at her own ankles, as if expecting to find she had a tattoo as well. "It's not permanent, I hope. A girl that pretty shouldn't disfigure herself. What's the point of it anyway?"

"Oh, you know, she's lonely for him and wants to show how she feels." In principle Eileen disapproved as much as Richard of the child's marring herself, but in fact she derived a vicarious pleasure from Jessica's lovelorn gesture, just as she did from the girl's general melancholy ever since Adam had left. A mother wasn't allowed to express her sense of loss so openly, without appearing unbalanced. Perhaps that was why she felt burdened by these weekend visits of Richard's. Not because she cherished her privacy, but because, by herself, there wasn't the strain of pretending she would ever feel quite whole again.

"She didn't seem all that lonely when I saw her," Richard said of Jessica. "The two sidekicks were with her."

"You mean Trip and Greg." Her husband always referred to them as "the sidekicks." They were good friends of Adam who'd decided to stay home and attend the local junior college. "I think it's nice," Eileen said, "the way Adam's crowd has stuck together, the ones who are still around." Was Richard implying something else? Did he suspect Trip and Greg of trying to move in on Adam's girl? What a peculiar man he was. The essence of his peculiarity, she thought, was his tendency to underestimate people's need for simple companionship. Everything with him was a struggle, a competition. Life was made up of hierarchies, chains of command. He had a son. His son had sidekicks, also a girlfriend. Where the latter was concerned, the sidekicks might or might not be loyal. That was the way Richard looked at things.

"Anyway," he told her, "the three of them said they just dropped by, they'd talk to you another time."

"They've been looking in on me occasionally. It's sort of sweet actually. I think they're worried about Adam's eccentric mother. You know, living by herself out here in the wilds."

"Our lady of the woods."

She smiled, though the comment stung her. "Is that what I am?"

To her surprise, he appeared to take the question seriously. "You seem a little detached."

She turned to the dogs. "He should see us during the week, shouldn't he, girls?" Santa and Diabla wagged their tails. "Why, sometimes we howl at the moon all night. We're not so ladylike when this man's not around, are we?"

"I've been thinking," he said. "We could close up the house for a while, live in Washington full time."

"No, Richard. Really." She would not discuss the subject. This place might be isolated, but it was home, the only one they'd lived in for more than three consecutive years during their entire marriage. She wasn't about to be uprooted again. Besides,

"Adam needs a permanent place to come back to," she said.

"I just thought—"

"I know it's hard on you," she said, "all this back-and-forth. You shouldn't think you have to fly down here every weekend on my account." Once out of her mouth, these words frightened her with how desolate they made her feel. Yet she meant them.

"This isn't about me, Eileen. I worry about you."

"You shouldn't," she said. "I'm doing fine here. Aren't we doing fine here, girls?"

"Please, stop talking to the dogs."

"Yes, sir."

"I didn't mean it that way," he said in a hurt tone.

"What way?"

"*Yes, sir.* I wasn't talking to you like that."

"I'm sorry, I thought you were."

SHE LIT SOME candles for extra light and they ate on the porch. "I invited Father Bernard to have dinner with us," she said, when they were halfway through the meal. "He couldn't come." Dinner, she knew, had disappointed Richard, and the news about Father Bernard was her way of saying, see, things could be worse. Her husband hadn't much use for the priest. "He was going square dancing at the VFW," she added.

"God, I hope he doesn't fall for some cowgirl." Father Bernard's predecessor had run off with a local woman a little more than a year ago, and ever since, Richard had been acting like a man betrayed.

"Well, you almost couldn't blame him if he did find someone," she said. "It must be awfully lonely for him, being the only priest for miles."

He looked at her in disbelief—his wife, the convert. Possibly he was wondering whether twenty years in the Church had been sufficiently transforming in her case. "I could blame him," he said.

"I'll tell you something else. How badly do you suppose he had to foul up his last assignment to get sent all the way down here?"

Eileen, too, had asked herself what a New Yorker like Bernard was doing in this backwater. You heard such disturbing stories about the clergy nowadays. But that didn't keep her from sympathizing with him in his exile; as the wife of a former officer, she knew what it was to be a stranger in a new place. Not that she'd had any intention of inviting the priest to dinner when she stopped by his little church on the way into town this afternoon. Sometimes she liked to visit Virgin Mary and the other statues, was all; she found it calming to sit in their presence, though it hadn't worked that way today. The impassive faces of the plaster figures had acted on her as an irritant—she'd begun to feel lately a bit like an effigy herself—and so she got up to leave soon after arriving. Father Bernard, as it happened, was just emerging from the devotional room near the back of the church; they walked together into the parking lot. That was when she asked him to dinner, feeling very forward in her invitation, because she could sense the priest's discomfort at being alone with her. Maybe it was the scandal created by his predecessor that made him anxious; maybe it was something about her. It was odd to think she might be giving off vibrations and not even be aware of it. In any case, his shyness made her bold. She was disappointed when he informed her he had other plans, was going dancing, of all things.

"You're smiling," Richard said.

"I was just picturing Father Bernard at a square dance."

"Very funny."

She didn't mention what was just as funny, that she'd been picturing Richard there as well—paired not with her (she was dancing with the priest) but with some pert thing in red flats who tossed her curls and twirled her petticoats around him.

He hated to dance. She supposed it was because, like most men, he dreaded making a fool of himself. You'd think at some age they'd get over that. But maybe it was part of their appeal, part of what drew you to them in the first place, that ego they were always protecting, like some military secret. That's how it had been with Richard and her anyway, in the beginning. As a young officer, he already exuded an air of absolute autonomy. Coming from a large and close-knit family herself, she was curious to know the reasons behind such singleness of character. And probably, too, in the pride of her youth, she felt challenged to break in on him in his solitude, never dreaming how difficult life with such a man—a man who didn't seem to need people—might be.

Soon after they were married, she'd begun taking instructions in the Catholic church and within a year converted from a lifelong, if tepid, Lutheranism. Perhaps religion had been her way of getting closer to him. And yet even within the bosom of his faith, he'd somehow eluded her. The Church called marriage a sacrament and regarded it as the only true vocation for the adult Christian outside the religious life. But when Adam was born, Eileen poured nearly everything into the child; it was motherhood more than matrimony that felt holy and ordained to her. No doubt she overdid it, got too wrapped up in the boy— and was paying for it now. Certainly with all the moving around the family did, mother and son had come to rely more than was normal on each other's company. She used to worry about suffocating him, but seeing the way he'd turned out—how many loyal friends he'd made in only three years here, how well he seemed to be adjusting to college—she thought she could stop worrying. Richard could stop, too. The boy was all right, she felt like assuring him. Better than all right; he'd become quite an impressive young man. His friends—Jessica, Trip, and Greg— were a little in awe of him, if the truth be known. Eileen sensed in them a certain wistfulness where Adam was concerned, as if they understood he was in the process of outgrowing them. It was a wistfulness she shared.

Richard pushed his chair back and crossed his legs. The dogs took this as a signal and came over to be petted. They stood on either side of him as he let his hands trail languorously down their backs. When he came to their tail bones, he scratched them there. The dogs' tongues came out, licking the air. "Come here, Santa," Eileen said, wanting one of them for herself, but Santa just rolled her eyes in the direction of her mistress, content to remain where she was. "Well, I like that," Eileen said, in mock irritation. "Some man comes along and you forget all about me."

Just beyond the screened porch the sound of crickets was deafening. Eileen's thoughts reverted to the injured deer outside. There was something patient and abiding about its presence in her woods. Almost reassuring. As if it were waiting for her. She didn't relish the idea of venturing out in the dark, picking her way through those dense trees. But when dinner was over she meant to do something, see if she could help the poor thing.

Richard said, "I saw a fellow who could have been Adam's twin in the Raleigh-Durham airport this afternoon." Perhaps she looked hopeful, because he added, "It wasn't him."

"Of course not. He would have called to say he was coming."

"Right, but for all I knew he had called and this fellow riding up in front of me on the escalator was him. I figured, what a coincidence, we're probably on the same flight. I mean, this guy looked just like Adam from the back. I started pushing my way up the escalator, calling his name. Guess I should have known something was wrong when he didn't turn around." Richard paused, shaking his head over this error of his. "Anyway, when I got up next to him I could see he was older than Adam. A young executive type—Adam five years from now. I must have been looking at him kind of funny, because he gave me this fish eye, like, who the hell are you?"

Eileen was thinking she'd never mistake anyone else for Adam, even from behind in a crowded airport. How many times had she lingered in doorways and at windows, watching his receding back as he headed off for school or the playground? She had done so too often to be fooled by an imposter, even for an instant. Still, what struck her was, Richard might have seen their son; it was in the realm of possibility. Her husband and son inhabited the same world now—a world of striving, of comings and goings—far removed from her own cloistered life here among the pines. So they might conceivably have run into each other at the airport, or elsewhere. And might yet. The chance of such a thing's happening caused a silent protest to rise within her. I'm the one who's out of it, she thought.

Richard shifted in his chair and cleared his throat, as if to bring her back from wherever she'd wandered to. "I know you miss him," he said. "I miss him, too."

"You do?"

"Sure. Of course, I do. What did you think?"

"I'm sorry. I guess ... I don't know what I thought. I'm sorry you miss him, too." He grimaced, apparently not wanting her sympathy. What did he want? What was he doing here in his white shirt, sitting on her back porch, in the candlelight? Beyond a sense of duty, what kept him returning every week?

After the dishes were cleared, he excused himself to go back to the guesthouse. "I won't be long," he told her, but she said not to hurry, she had some things to attend to herself.

When she was sure he was settled out there, she shut the dogs up in the house so they wouldn't make a fuss, retrieved a flashlight from her car, and walked up the driveway to where she'd first seen the deer this afternoon. She shone the light through the trees and after some searching spotted the animal, lying in the same position as before. She turned off the light so as not to frighten it.

It was so dark in the woods she had to proceed like a sleep-walker, with her arms extended in front of her, to avoid bumping into the trees. "It's okay, I'm not going to hurt you," she kept repeating softly, assuming the deer must be terrified at the sound of her footsteps. She stumbled once but caught herself. Another time she scraped her shoulder against some bark. "Ouch!" She touched her sleeve; it was sticky. Blood? No, probably pine sap. "It's okay," she said, peering into the darkness. "It's okay." She guessed she must be very near the spot. She listened but heard nothing stirring. She switched on the flashlight, aiming it up into the branches so as not to startle the animal with a direct beam; the light reflecting downward from the trees might be enough to help her find what she was looking for. And so it was. The deer lay not five yards from her. She knelt down; the ground was soft with pine needles. The dim shape in front of her appeared rigid with fear, utterly petrified. What had Richard said? They hold still to keep from being seen. The creature's instinct for self-preservation made her heart ache. She leaned forward, holding out a hand, wondering, are deer anything like dogs, can they smell good intentions? "Are you okay? Are you?" She reached the final few inches and touched its muzzle, then snatched her hand back. Grabbing up the flashlight and aiming it directly at the animal's face, she was met with a look of mournful distress such as she might have expected, but exaggerated beyond nature—a plaster parody of distress, with even a tear painted in the corner of one large and doleful eye. Her deer was a fraud.

"Oh!" she gasped, and glanced around her, half thinking this must be a practical joke; there must be people hiding behind these trees laughing at her. But it was more than the embarrassment of the moment that affected her. She felt as if the loneliness and desolation she'd been keeping to herself, which had all but consumed her in the past few weeks, were now exposed and held up to ridicule. It was cruel, cruel. She clambered to her feet and ran back toward the driveway, the flashlight swinging at her side, its random beam raking the tree trunks. The ground felt as if it were tilting beneath her.

She hit the tree hard. She did not know she hit it. All at once she was lying on her back in an open meadow, squinting up at the sun. Or so it seemed. She did not know how she came to be in that place, except she was dimly aware there'd been a mishap and it was her fault. Had she fallen asleep while driving, run the car into a ditch, and been thrown clear? She tried to sit up but couldn't. I'm hurt, she thought. It was a matter-of-fact observation, such as a doctor or nurse might make. Adam appeared, standing over her. He wore a baseball cap, the bill frayed; he couldn't have been more than ten. Santa and Diabla were with him. Eileen thanked God she had not been responsible for harming her son, that he'd come through the accident unscathed. She wished he would not look so worried, though. And the dogs, too. They were all gazing down at her, their innocent faces etched with concern. She tried to move her lips to reassure them but nothing came out. "I'll go get Dad," Adam said. "He can help you." She tried to sit up again, to tell him it wasn't necessary, she had everything she needed right here, everything in the world. "I'm going now," he said. "I'm going to get Dad."

With a tremendous effort of will, Eileen sat up. As she did so, all the light drained from her head and she was in the pine forest. "Ohhh," she cried, hugging herself and rocking back-and-forth.

She stopped rocking after a while. What was that sound? It wasn't crickets; it was more shrill than crickets, so high-pitched as to be nearly inaudible, like one of those whistles only dogs can detect. She put her hands over her ears but could still hear it.

When she made it back to the house, Santa and Diabla were sleeping soundly, curled next to each other under the kitchen table. She left them undisturbed and limped upstairs to the bathroom. The sight of herself in the mirror made her wince, then it almost made her laugh. Pine needles clung to her hair, sticking out at angles, like pins from a cushion; her blouse was ripped at the shoulder; and there were scrapes and bruises on her forehead and on one knee. She looked like the mad woman of the forest.

At least she hadn't broken anything or suffered internal injuries, unless that remote shrillness in her head signified something amiss up there. Oddly enough, she didn't mind the sound; it had the effect of clearing her mind and helping her to focus. Perhaps that was why she now recalled a conversation with Jessica a couple weeks ago in which the girl had mentioned a piece of discarded statuary in her parents' garage—a deer. Jessica claimed real deer were sometimes attracted by life-like replicas; would Eileen like to have it? So that's what the three kids had been doing here this afternoon when Richard happened on them.

Her husband would have a funny story to tell about his wife back in Washington. Who would he tell it to? she wondered. A friend or a colleague, a man or a woman? She couldn't begin to imagine. But the thought of his confiding the tale of her folly to another woman, one who would listen with just the right mixture of appreciation and sympathy, as only an interested female knew how to do, made her angry, and also jealous. If she thought he would do that, talk about her to another woman, if she thought it for a minute, she would go back outside right now, dispose of the plaster deer somehow, and make up a story about her injuries. Returning to those woods was the last thing she wanted to do, but she could do it. She'd become, over the years, just as adept at hiding herself from him as he was from her. What a pair they were! What an expanse now stretched between them; it could not be measured in the number of steps from here to the guesthouse, or even in the number of miles from here to Washington.

Was that the door she heard downstairs? The dog whistle in her head had all her nerves tuned to a keen pitch. Santa and Diabla were stirring; she could hear their claws skittering over the kitchen floor and could picture them dancing in welcome around Richard. They gave two sharp, joyous barks, as if to announce his arrival. Eileen looked in the mirror. She was a mess, a mess! And he would be here in a minute. She thought of him in his white shirt, making his way toward her through the dark house.

CONFLICTING FORECASTS

Alton's father sidled up to the mannequin and snapped the elastic in her briefs. Jockey shorts for women. The old man couldn't get over it. "You ought to take a pair home to Robin," he joked.

Alton didn't tell him Robin already owned several pairs, that it was no big deal, especially under the circumstances. He didn't think he should have to tell him. Alton's mother, over in flannel robes, was heaving sighs the shoppers could hear out on the promenade.

Not that his father noticed. The only saleswoman in the department had attached herself to him. "Not very feminine, are they?" she said, referring to the Jockey shorts. She was about the old man's age and wore an ankle bracelet. They smiled at each other, of one mind on the subject of lady's underwear. She was wearing a button that said "Join Our Intimate Apparel Club," and Alton half expected his father to ask about the terms of membership.

At the saleswoman's urging, the old man picked out a peach satin nightgown and took it over to his wife. Alton couldn't bring himself to look but could hear plainly enough. "What's wrong with you, Forrest?" she said, her voice trembling. "You act like I'm going to a pajama party."

Alton's father returned the nightgown to the saleswoman, holding its limpness in his outstretched hands as if it had been a live thing he hadn't meant to harm. Alton didn't blame his mother. She was angry and frightened, and his father always mistook the occasion. But why had she dragged them here anyway? To their third lingerie department tonight? Was she searching, on the eve of her surgery, for something appropriate to die in? And who could live at such a pitch for very long?

NOT THE REST of the world, that was for sure. Apart from Alton, and of course his mother, nobody seemed to appreciate the gravity of this crisis. When his father called with the news, Robin hadn't been able to get the message straight at first. She'd been waiting for word that a friend in Idaho had given birth, and as soon as she heard the crackle of long distance it was this happy news she expected to hear. The old man, never very good at conveying alarm, had a hard time making her understand that he was not announcing a birth but calling to say Alton's mother needed cancer surgery.

Robin got right to work on an airline ticket. "If you take the flight that leaves before 7 a.m. and stay at least five days," she told Alton, "you can get the Super-Saver Fare." He found comforting her knack for reducing nearly any problem to a matter of logistics. Last year she'd guided him without incident through airports, train stations, and subways in five European countries. "Your mother will be all right," she said, kissing him at the airport. "You wait and see."

The woman next to him on the plane said that several years ago she had the same surgery as Alton's mother. "I believe things like this are nature's way of telling us to take better care of ourselves," the woman said. "I'm healthier now than I ever was before."

Along the plane's narrow, lurching aisle, the stewardesses balanced breakfast trays with casual efficiency, oblivious to the fact they were walking a high wire six miles up. With their short, feathery haircuts and colorful blouses, they made Alton consider the birds of the air and the lilies of the fields. Everything about the stewardesses—even their beauty, which was not heartbreaking—seemed calculated to assure him and the other passengers no calamity could befall them.

Alton wondered, if enough people feel everything will be all right, is it just possible everything will be all right? The streaks of lightning in the clouds over his hometown said no. So did the stricken look on his mother's face when she met him at the gate. "I've really done it this time," she said. It was as if she believed tumors grew from a defect of will.

"You should take another relaxing pill when we get home," Alton's father told her on the way back from the airport.

"That's his solution," she told Alton. "I should go to sleep."

"She won't even try to relax," his father said.

"Your father doesn't understand it's hard to relax when you're in limbo."

"Of course, it's hard," Alton said. "At least we'll know something soon."

When they turned down the hill that led to their house, the old man called out, "There's the bridge." It was the family landmark, a white, wooden arch spanning the creek in front of their home. "What do you think, is this the place?"

"This is it," said Alton's mother, always grateful to find herself safely back where she started from.

"Alton? Turn in here?"

"For heaven's sake, Forrest!" Alton's mother said. "Turn in before you miss it."

ALTON'S MOTHER AGREED to take a sedative and lie down after lunch, but only if she could watch the soap operas. Alton watched with her. Two women were sitting on a patio drinking iced tea, regretting the passing of a close friend. "What you're both really concerned about," Alton's mother said to the women on TV, "is hopping into bed with your dead friend's husband."

"Life goes on," sighed one of the women, as if answering her. Alton and his mother had to laugh. Pretty soon a weather bulletin flashed on the screen.

"I was just outside," said Alton's father, poking his head in. "It's clearing off."

When he was gone, Alton's mother said, "You check."

Alton went out and stood on the bridge. He used to fish for crawdads here, watching for their tiny, darting shadows under the water. He posed for birthday and graduation pictures here, too, squinting into the future. So it seemed fitting to him—and more than a little portentous—to be standing now in the same spot, scanning the autumn horizon on his mother's behalf.

"It might be a little dark over in the west," he reported back to her. This seemed to satisfy her.

"Are you and Robin suffering terribly with the heat down there?"

"We like hot weather, Mom."

"Madeleine Carson's son is stationed there. He found a scorpion in his shower." Eventually she dozed off but not for long. "Oh, that was the craziest dream," she said, but wouldn't tell him what it was about.

The old man came in again. "Well?" Alton's mother said. He allowed as how it was getting a little darker in the west.

"We'll have to go to the basement," she said, though she made no move in that direction.

"I CAN'T BELIEVE I slept through the storm," Alton's mother said in the morning. Limbs were down in the yard. The old man winked at Alton. The pills had worked.

In the afternoon they drove to the radiologist's for a bone scan. "We used to come out this way to buy eggs," said Alton's father. "You remember?"

"I remember Billy Butthead," Alton said.

Billy Butthead had been the goat that belonged to the farmer who sold eggs. The animal used to chase Alton and his sister back and forth between the car and the farmhouse. He would chase them right up the porch steps and butt his head against the screen door after they slammed it behind them. Then he'd glare at them through the screen with his red eyes as they panted and giggled on the other side. The goat never got them, though he'd always seemed just about to. Alton and his sister had been deathly afraid of him and always looked forward to their trips to the farm.

"Good old Billy Butthead," the old man said.

The bone scan took only a few minutes, but then they had to wait in the office to hear the results. The doctor who conducted the test, Alton's mother told them, was eight months pregnant. She wore a double lead vest to protect the baby from radiation. "She was awfully kind to me," Alton's mother said.

When the pregnant radiologist came out, she said there was no evidence the cancer had spread to the bone.

"You see?" Alton's father said to his mother.

His mother was so relieved tears came into her eyes. "Thank you," she said to the doctor. "Good luck with the baby."

"Everything's going to be fine," said the doctor.

"I don't know, I'm such a big coward."

"No, you're not."

"No, I'm really not."

"Things hit her harder than most people," the old man said.

"What she's going through would hit anyone hard," Alton said.

"My son understands," said his mother to the doctor. "He's the same way. Neither of us can take things in stride."

She slept on the way home. When she woke up, she said, "Alton, I think you should call your sister and let her know I'm having surgery tomorrow."

His mother and sister had not spoken for two years, not since his sister eloped to California with a divorced man. Before she left, there had been some bad scenes, including one in which Alton's mother picked up a butcher knife and threatened to harm herself if Alton's sister didn't give up the man.

When Alton called to tell his sister about the operation, she said, "I know all about it. Daddy's been keeping me posted. He says not to get all upset."

"He doesn't want to face it. This is serious."

"Don't start on me, Alton. I'm not flying back there."

"Nobody's asking you to. Mom just thought you should know what was happening."

"I know, she's got this big scene worked out in her mind— the grieving family around her bed. She won't be happy until she gets herself and everyone else whipped into a frenzy."

"We had the bone scan today."

"And?" Alton paused. He wanted to make his sister wait for the good news.

"Tell me, Alton. It's bad, isn't it?"

Now he was ashamed of himself. "No, it was all clear."

"You creep," she said. "Such a little ghoul. You and Mother. Tell me, were the two of you so disappointed with the good news you had to call up and see if you could get a rise out of me? Was that it, Alton?"

"I think she misses you, if you want to know."

"I'm not listening to this."

Alton's sister didn't want to believe in crisis and tragedy anymore. Not that she hadn't had her share. She and the man she ran off with hadn't married after all. And she later confessed to Robin she ended up getting an abortion. Since then she'd had her tubes tied and was now living with a rich orthodontist. She insisted she was content in her new life but Alton doubted it. Happiness was a goal his sister pursued with more determination than aptitude.

"We were talking today," he told her. "Do you remember driving out to get eggs and that goat that used to—"

"Billy Butthead! That monster still turns up in my dreams. Do you believe Mother, with her imagination for catastrophe, letting that animal traumatize her children?"

"The goat never even touched us. It was fun."

"Fun nothing."

"Well, there's not even a farm there anymore, so you can stop being traumatized."

"Just think, old Billy Butthead."

As THEY BACKED out of the driveway on the morning of the operation, Alton's mother said, "How will I go on if they find something really bad?" Alton in the back seat couldn't imagine what to say. He was wondering the same thing. How would she go on?

"Did you take the pill?" the old man asked her.

"Oh, shut up, Forrest," she snapped.

Alton's father didn't even flinch. He drove with one hand on the wheel. Alton could see, by leaning forward, that with the other hand his father was patting her knee. After a while his mother took the hand in both of hers and held it.

At the hospital the nurses and orderlies started preparing her for surgery. "Upsy-daisy."

"We're going to make you woozy now." They treated her, Alton thought, exactly as if she were ten years old and in for tonsils.

The mood changed after the two priests arrived. Everyone stepped back from the gurney on which Alton's mother was lying. One priest, the hospital chaplain, wore a gold filigree medallion studded with jewels. He undid a clasp on the medallion and removed a Host, placing it on Alton's mother's tongue. The other priest, her pastor, anointed her with oils.

When the ceremony was completed, Alton's mother smiled serenely at those gathered around. There was consolation, after all, she seemed to say, in preparing for the worst. "I'm a little warm," she said. One of the female cousins sprang forward and began fanning her with a newspaper. A nurse gave an orderly the sign, and Alton's mother went gliding off with her entourage.

SOME OF THE family passed the time watching soaps in the waiting room. "Your mother will want to know what happens," Alton's aunt said. "Friday's always the big day on these programs."

Even as she spoke a distinguished looking man up on the screen was explaining to a young woman that her mother had not perished in an airplane crash after all. Unknown to anyone, the once headstrong mother had been living among them these many months, a reformed person, now wise in acquiescence, a sort of fairy godmother to them all. "How is it possible?" the young woman naturally wanted to know. "Reconstructive surgery," said the distinguished looking man. "A miracle of science."

Alton's aunt asked if he and Robin were just burning up where they lived. "Everybody has air conditioning," he said. "The neighbors on both sides have pools. It's very comfortable."

"I read somewhere it's the first place they'd bomb in a nuclear war," his aunt said.

Alton said he needed to call Robin.

"I don't have any news," he told his wife. "I just wanted to talk to you."

"Oh, sweetie, how are all of you holding up?"

"We're all right. What are you doing?" She sounded out of breath.

"I ran in from outside. I was digging in the flower bed. Boy, is it hot."

"Is it?"

"As blazes."

"You won't get heat stroke, will you, or let a scorpion sting you?"

"What? Oh. It's been like that, has it?"

"I'll survive."

"I know you will. It's your sister I'm worried about. She called. She's in a state. You shouldn't have tried to upset her."

"She'll be all right. Her dentist boy friend can give her laughing gas and she won't feel a thing."

"You're not very nice. Think how terrible it's going to be for her if your mother is terminal."

"It's not going to come to that."

"I know it's not. I'm sorry I said that. I guess talking to your sister's got me in a state, too."

"Don't you go nuts on me," he said.

"Come home soon, then."

"I'll call you when we know anything."

"Call your sister first. She's waiting by the phone."

"Okay."

"And be kind."

BACK IN THE waiting room the windows had gone blind with rain. "Hope you don't flood, Forrest," somebody said to Alton's father. The creek in front of the house had been known to overflow its banks in hard rains. The old man looked out the window. "It's barely coming down," he said. Everyone smiled. Alton's father never thought the house would flood. He liked to remind people of the time his wife, alarmed by predictions of widespread flooding, insisted they move all the family possessions to the second floor. Scarcely a drop of rain had fallen.

In rebuttal, Alton's mother would trot out the photograph she once took of her son standing in the toilet, wearing a martyr's expression, as he tried to stem the rising tide of sewer water. "The whole family had to be inoculated," she said, aiming a look of infinite reproach at the old man. "Oh, that creek of his!" She had convinced herself over the years it was her husband's fault they lived next to the creek at all, though she would never have considered moving.

"There's one thing she likes about that creek," Alton's father was fond of saying. "The bridge."

"Yes, that's true," Alton's mother had to admit.

In the beginning she said the bridge was ugly and she could not live with it; its curvature was too extreme. "It looks like a cat arching its back," she claimed. But Alton's father would not tear it down. He built it and he wanted to keep it. "You'll get used to it," he told her.

But she didn't, not right away. She would lie awake, she later admitted, thinking about the bridge with its arched back, how ugly it was and how she hated having it in front of her house. Once in the middle of the night she stole outside with a box of matches, struck off the whole box, one match after another, standing in her nightgown at the edge of the creek—but the bridge would not catch fire.

The old man always roared with delight when she told this on herself. "I knew in time she'd get used to it," he said, "if the bridge could survive."

Wonder of wonders, in time, she did get used to it. As the shrubs and trees Alton's father planted around the bridge began to fill out, they helped relieve its starkness. The bridge gradually settled into its surroundings, and not only settled in, but grew to be picturesque.

"You know what?" the old man would say. "When that bridge finally got rickety and had to be replaced, she wanted me to build another one just like it. 'You mean with a steep arch, like a cat's back?' I said. And she said, 'Exactly the same.'"

WHEN THE SURGEON came into the waiting room, Alton's father got to his feet a little unsteadily to receive the news. The surgeon had a name that sounded like "Munchkin," which suited his small stature, as well as his bushy red eyebrows and mutton chop sideburns. He was supposed to be the best in his field, but standing there surrounded by the family, still in his scrubs, he possessed the air of a man who had strayed into the wrong part of the hospital. He said, in a voice so soft Alton had to strain to hear it, that he believed they managed to get all the cancer, they would have to study the lab results, chemotherapy might or might not be indicated. The surgeon seemed a little embarrassed when the old man insisted on shaking his hand.

"So what does it mean?" Alton's aunt asked, after the doctor had gone. "Is she going to be okay?"

"I don't know," said Alton's father, dropping back into his chair. "I guess we'll have to wait."

Alton and his father were waiting in his mother's room when they wheeled her in. She seemed very small under the sheets, as if they had cut a good portion of her away. "Oh, hi," she said, acting like it was a charming coincidence, finding her husband and son there. She was still half asleep, pleasantly suspended, drifting on a current of anesthetic and painkillers. It did not occur to her to wonder why her daughter was not there, how the operation had gone, or whether she would live or die. These questions, Alton knew, would come later, and with great urgency. His mother would have to learn to live with them. They all would.

"Look at the flowers," the old man was urging her.

"Let her sleep, Dad."

"No, she needs to be awake now," the nurse said.

"Look at these Patient Lucys from Mrs. Hale," the old man insisted. Her eyelids fluttered as he rattled off the names of other plants and people.

Alton pictured Robin down on her hands and knees digging in the steamy earth of their new home. He wanted to call her but had promised to call his sister first. Robin had said to be kind. But how could he be kind when the news was so equivocal?

Later they brought some broth and toast for his mother. She wasn't hungry but they wanted her to eat something. "I'll be back in a minute, Dad," Alton said. The old man didn't hear. He was dipping the toast in the broth and feeding it to his wife, a little at a time.

Alton had a clear image of his sister as he dialed her number. When he and Robin talked to her, she often said, "Oh, I'm just sitting here by the pool. Can you hear the water lapping?" She referred to her boyfriend's "Olympic-size" pool. "I tell you guys, I feel like I've died and gone to heaven."

"When the big earthquake hits," Alton once told her, "heaven's not the direction you'll be headed." He imagined her sitting by the pool in California right now, though she would be less attuned to the sound of lapping water than to tremors in the earth, the ringing of a telephone.

"Hello?" she said, after only one ring. He could tell from the edge in her voice—so like their mother's—how alarming the sound of the phone must have been to her. He wondered if she was alone. Maybe the dentist was with her. He hoped so.

"Alton? How is everything?"

He took a deep breath. "Sis," he began, "everything is going to be all right."

COMPANION

She's not used to having him around in the daytime. Now and then, turning a corner, or glancing up as she enters a room, she's so startled to find she's not alone that her hand flies up to her heart and she lets out a gasp, imagining for the moment he's an intruder. About the third time this happens, he says, "For God's sake, Angela, it's me. Who did you think?" Then he stomps out of the house.

She's sorry she hurt his feelings; a husband has a right not to be treated like a stranger in his own home. Still, it's a relief not to have him underfoot, if only for a little while. She hopes he'll take the car, drive to the mall, go on one of his indoor walks. He knows some people there, other walkers.

Is it her responsibility to keep him entertained? Now that he's retired he seems to think so. Brochures displaying everything from the sands of Oahu to the skyscrapers of Hong Kong litter his night stand, like silent reproaches. Angela will not fly. "The only way I would get on an airplane," she tells him, "is if it's a medical emergency and one of the kids needs me. Even then it would take a couple glasses of wine."

Apparently her comment about the wine starts him thinking. He proposes several elaborate travel schemes, all hinging on his ability to render her unconscious. Sometimes he leans toward pills to get the job done, but recently he checked out a book from the library called *Your Hypnotic Powers*. Honestly, being married to him, she thinks, is like living with a child. "You could go to sleep in the airport," he says, "and wake up under the palm trees." His eyes are alight with the prospect of working such an enchantment.

"Why don't you just hit me over the head with a hammer, Forrest? That should do the trick." He, of all people, should know what a worrier she is. She could never relax on a vacation such as the one he's proposing. "There are people who depend on me," she says. Surely she doesn't have to recite for him the long list of friends, relatives, neighbors, and members of the parish to whom she contributes time and attention. Last year the bishop recognized her as the outstanding layperson. "Do-gooder's award," Forrest called it. According to him, she does too much, and from a health standpoint maybe he's right. Twice she's been operated on for cancer, and though the last time was three years ago, the doctors have yet to pronounce her completely cured.

"Call Sissy," she says, "ask her to go to Mambo Bambo or wherever with you." Their daughter, she suspects, is the one who's been encouraging him in these plans anyway. Sissy likes to tell anyone who'll listen that her father has earned "the right to enjoy himself"; she seems convinced her mother wants to prevent this from happening.

"Maybe I *will* call her," he says, as if this is a new idea for him. Angela's seen the long-distance bill and knows the two of them have been talking behind her back.

WHEN THE LADY whose job it is to take Communion to the sick and shut-ins of the parish decides to visit her niece in Florida for the winter, the priest asks Angela to take her place.

"It's only temporary," she assures Forrest, who rolls his eyes. "It's really a sort of honor to be asked. And when I'm finished, we could drive down to the lake for a few days. Spring is so pretty there."

"We'll see," he says. He's sitting by the picture window in her kitchen where he spends more and more of his time lately. Angela thinks it's sad for a man his age to be at such loose ends, as if he hadn't any more idea than a twenty year old where true contentment lies. She's tried involving him in the church, but he's never shown much interest in the life of the spirit. To her chagrin, he remains unbaptized after all these years and rarely accompanies her to Mass. When they married, she regarded his unbelief as a challenge, a cross to bear; she had taken up the burden eagerly, confident of his eventual conversion. Now she wonders if it's heresy to accept that certain people—earthbound people—simply lack the religious impulse. To her son and daughter, whom she raised strictly in the faith, she used to say about their father, "There are many ways of being good and serving God. Your father is a good man in his way." And, truly, she believes this.

"You like the lake," she reminds him. "Remember what fun you had fishing with Harold Gray?"

"Mmm."

Harold Gray is an unfortunate reference. Two years ago he ran a plastic hose from his car's exhaust to the window and died. The police told Forrest that people who attempt suicide in this way usually botch the job. But Harold always knew how to do things. Just like Forrest. She studies him as he sits in the window, watching the birds at the big feeder he built in the back yard last year. There's not much to see out there; all the colorful birds are gone. After a summer and fall of being bullied by blue jays, the drab sparrows and starlings finally have the yard to themselves, though it's sad to think what a cold price they pay for the privilege.

What's going on in her husband's head? she wonders. What, for example, is behind this sudden urge to travel? She could shoot Sissy, first getting him all excited about a trip, then begging off when he asked her to go with him. Not that Forrest would ever blame the girl, who claims she's in the middle of studying for her real estate license. According to their daughter, there's a property boom in New Mexico, where she lives, and she wants in on it.

"She's got a new boyfriend," Angela says. "I'll bet you."

Forrest regards her blandly, like a man who doesn't need to bet. She realizes he's got some further piece of news from Sissy— a hot flash from the Land of Enchantment—and is trying to decide whether or not to let his wife in on it. "She did mention someone," he allows.

"Tell me he doesn't make pottery and live in a mud hut."

"As a matter of fact, he's got his own business. Land sales, I think she said."

"That explains the real estate license, doesn't it? When will that girl learn? A man doesn't want a woman who tries to be involved in every part of his life."

"Some men might."

"Why, Forrest, you know perfectly well you would have hated it if I'd tried poking around in your business affairs."

He shrugs, meaning he knows she's right but won't give her the pleasure of owning up to it.

"It's the truth and you know it," she says. "You took care of business, and I took care of the house. That's the way we did things."

SHE TELLS HIM about the sick people she's been visiting, the ones she takes Communion to. "The way some of them tip their heads back and open their mouths to be fed," Angela says, "makes me think of baby birds."

"You don't say." She's not surprised he mistakes her remark as an expression of sentimental piety. "Meals on wheels for Catholics," that's how he refers to her new job. Still, she tries to keep in mind what a nun once told her: "It's not for you or me to know what word or gesture might drop into the heart of the unbeliever and take hold there." She's always done her best to set a good example for her husband, though that wasn't her intention just now. Rather she'd been picturing her newest flock, the wheelchair-bound and bedridden communicants whose faces have begun to crowd her thoughts at night before she falls asleep. They close in on her—their bruised-looking eyes shut tight, mouths gaping, necks straining, in attitudes of almost rapt hunger, unlike anything she's experienced as a Eucharistic minister in church, where the faithful wear devotion as if it were a mask. Angela supposes she should feel uplifted by the undisguised yearning she's witnessed in hospitals and sickrooms; it should be one of the rewards of the job. Instead she finds it vaguely unsettling.

"I have to read their charts," she tells him, "because some of them try to receive Communion when they aren't able to swallow. They end up choking."

This seems to interest him as a practical matter. "You should try breaking off a little piece of the bread and dipping it in water. Then it would slide down their throats."

She could have used his advice the other day. A man with tubes running in and out of his body had coughed up the consecrated Host. There it lay in a soggy wad on his chest, soaking through his hospital gown. She didn't know what to do, so she grabbed some Kleenex from a dispenser beside his bed, scooped up the mess, and deposited it in her purse, fighting back the urge to gag. "It's all right," she assured the mortified patient, "these things happen." When she got back to the parish rectory, she handed over the Kleenex with the Host to the priest, who dropped it unceremoniously into the trash. "Don't worry," he said to a surprised Angela, "our Lord is used to traveling anywhere."

She wishes He hadn't traveled in her purse, however. It'll have to be thrown away, along with most of its contents, because there's no telling what disease that patient might have been carrying. "I wish I were a better person," she tells Forrest, "but I can't help it—being around all these sick people makes me nervous about my own health. For one thing, I keep imagining the cancer's coming back."

"You should quit," he says.

Of course. Every problem, he seems to believe, has a pat solution. Afraid to fly? Take a sedative. Afraid of death? Don't think about it. The only problem he can't solve is the problem of his wife. That one appears to have him completely baffled. "You don't listen," he sometimes tells her. "You don't listen worth a damn." She assumes what he means is, you don't listen to me. Anyway, she has no intention of quitting her new job.

One morning when she gets up he's waiting for her at the kitchen table with a map of the city spread out in front of him. Based on what he's been able to put together of her recent visits to hospitals, nursing homes, and private residences, he claims she could plan her itinerary more efficiently, thus saving time and gasoline. "Look here," he says, "you've been going like this—in a zigzag. Why not take 435 toward Lee Summit, then swing north on the traffic way?" With a yellow marker, he traces a wide arc on the map.

"Okay," she says. The simplicity of the plan appeals to her. "Fold it up and leave it next to my purse."

"Just look at it," he says. "Doesn't this make better sense than what you've been doing?"

"I believe you," she says, going to get the milk for their cereal.

"But look at what you were doing!" Apparently, the more he studies the map the more her stupidity amazes him.

"I'm in a hurry, Forrest. Show me later."

He's shaking his head over the map. "Zigzag, zigzag."

"I get around just fine, I'll have you know."

"Like a chicken with its head cut off."

"Will you just be quiet?"

"Like a damned ninny!"

"For heaven's sake, Forrest! What difference does it make which way I go as long as I get there?"

"Fine, you do it your way."

When she's ready to leave, he's nowhere in sight and neither is his map. All right, she thinks, he's got his feelings hurt again, though the unfairness of his doing so makes her mad. Didn't all the insulting things that were said come straight from him? She must remember to tell her son about this incident next time they talk on the phone, sometime when Forrest is not around. Her son, Alton, unlike his sister, still recalls how aggravating their father, and his moods, can be. "Your father's almost seventy-one," she'll tell him, "and all of a sudden he's as touchy as a new bride."

THE END OF the day finds her returning from a far-flung suburb of the parish with darkness coming on and a light rain falling. The rain may be changing to ice on her windshield, but probably that's her imagination. She thinks of pulling into a gas station and calling Forrest to tell him dinner's going to be late. She won't though. She can hear him now: "You're where? What are you doing way out there?" She already knows she made a mistake; it would have been more practical to head this direction first, then work her way back home. Why can she never think of such things beforehand? "Because you're too busy all the time." Forrest's voice comes to her unbidden, as clearly as if he were sitting beside her. "Busy, busy, busy." The word buzzes around in her head, mocking all her good works.

It's been an upsetting day. First there was her visit to the cancer floor where it always frightens her to go. All she wants to do in that place is escape. Today she gave Communion to a man not much older than her son. He had a smudge on his cheek the color of a blackberry; it looked harmless, like someone's careless thumbprint. Bending over him, she felt the urge to wet a handkerchief and rub it off. But she knew better. One of the nurses had told her: melanoma.

Even more disturbing was the home call she paid to the Wetzels in the afternoon. Angela had not seen Greta Wetzel at Mass for some time but remembered her as a big, bustling woman— a good worker when she served on the church cleaning committee, though determined to do things her own way and inclined to go off in a sulk if anyone crossed her. Now, dying of emphysema, she must have felt life itself had crossed her; she had fallen into a permanent sulk, punctuated by fits of anger. This much Angela gathered from the husband, who arranged for the visit.

"Does she want to receive the Eucharist?" Angela had asked.

"Oh, yes," he assured her.

Nevertheless, when Angela pronounced the words—"Body of Christ"—and offered the Host to Mrs. Wetzel, she flatly refused it. "No," the sick woman said, shaking her head slowly back and forth, "no."

Angela, Host in hand, remained frozen in a posture of bestowal. She had never seen anyone reject Communion before.

"Greta, please, don't do this," her husband said.

"No, take it away, I don't want it." The woman's eyes were ablaze, her chest heaved with the effort of breathing. Though she was weak and horribly shrunken from her former self, a powerful negative energy clung to her and lent authority to her words. Lying there, she made a sort of spectacle, at once fascinating and appalling, like one of those dying planets or doomed stars Angela had read about, which instead of exploding or cooling gradually, collapses in on itself and smolders.

Mr. Wetzel apologized to Angela at the front door. "I shouldn't have brought you out here. It's just that, well, I thought if the opportunity was presented, she might give in."

"Of course, it was worth a try," she said, trying not to let him see how the episode had shaken her.

"You shouldn't take it personally," he said. "She acts that way to spite me. She's mad because I won't give her cigarettes. You believe that? Smoking's what got her in this fix to begin with. I tell you, there's not a more stubborn woman in the world."

Is it Angela's imagination or had Mr. Wetzel's distress over his wife's obstinacy been colored by a certain pride? Oh, well, let the poor man find solace where he can. As for her, it seems she's been skirting death all day—snagged in its orbit—zigzag how she will. Now she only wants to get home. She would even be grateful for someone to tell her the best route.

NEXT MORNING FORREST sits by the picture window reading the newspaper. "It's supposed to be seventy degrees in Albuquerque today," he says.

"Sissy must miss the change of seasons living in a place like that," Angela says. "Spring wouldn't be anything special to look forward to."

"San Antonio's going to get up to eighty-three," he says.

"Oh, that's just too hot for this time of year. Don't you think? I wouldn't like that."

"Eighty-three and sunny, it says."

"I hope Alton's protecting himself against the ultraviolet rays." The next time she talks to her son and his wife she means to tell them about the young man she saw in the hospital the other day.

"It was ninety-one in Needles, California, yesterday. Ninety-one!"

"Mmm." Her thoughts are still scattered between Texas and New Mexico. What does she care about Needles? They have no child in Needles, thank God. She doesn't like to think of Sissy and Alton living so far away, and in places so different from where they were brought up. Sometimes she wonders if the spots they've chosen don't amount to a tacit rejection of home.

Forrest, meanwhile, has left the temperate climes and is forging his way toward the arctic rim. "International Falls: seventeen degrees and snow," he reports. "Eau Claire: nine degrees and wind gusts up to forty miles per hour." Next she'll have to hear about the natural disasters—flooding in the Northwest, mudslides in Southern California. Then maybe he'll favor her with an astrological forecast. The stars say, you are going on a long journey. Ha.

His parents and both sets of grandparents were farmers, and Angela supposes that's why he's always been fascinated with the elements. But to her, talk of the weather ranks just above whistling or chewing gum as a means of passing the time. "What about here, Forrest?" she interrupts. "What's our forecast?"

"I did that already," he says. "You weren't paying attention. Mid-thirties, chance of snow showers."

"And I have to go all the way to Gladstone."

"You should take the by-pass, get off just after the river."

When she's ready to leave, he's still at the window with the paper. She has an idea. "Why don't you drive me today? Make yourself useful."

He laughs silently at her jab but doesn't budge.

"I'm serious, Forrest. You know I don't like it when the streets are bad. C'mon, or can't you drag yourself out of that rocking chair?"

"I'm ready," he says, putting down the paper and clapping his hands on his knees. "You ready?"

"I'm standing here in my coat, Forrest."

"Let's go."

AFTER THAT HE doesn't wait to be invited. Whenever it's time to leave, he's already in the car, warming it up. For better or worse, it looks like she's got a driver.

Despite his earlier admonitions to take the simplest, most direct routes, he himself prefers unbeaten paths, she notices. He delights in confusing and surprising her. "Know where we are?" he'll ask. Often she doesn't. Then they'll turn a corner or crest a hill, and all of a sudden, right in front of her, there's a well-known landmark—St. Joseph's Hospital, the Stone Arch Bridge, the old Monkey Ward's building—but looking unfamiliar somehow, because they've approached it from a different angle. "Now do you know where you are?" he'll say, as pleased with himself as if he's conjured the scene before them out of thin air.

Sometimes even he gets confused as to their whereabouts. Or so she suspects. "Admit it, Forrest, you're lost. I'll never make it to Mrs. Reilly's by two o'clock!" A twitch of his shoulders, a slight adjustment of his seating position, these are the only hints she might be right. Otherwise, to look at him, you'd think he had all day to get where they're going. He drives slouched in his seat, his left shoulder up against the door, one hand lightly fingering the wheel, lips pursed in a soundless whistle—everything about him calculated to frustrate her own sense of urgency. "What's the big hurry?" That's his attitude. "With your clientele, it's not like they're going anywhere." Then he reminds her they haven't been late for an appointment yet, which is true. Her days are much better regulated since Forrest took over the driving.

He waits without complaint in the lobbies of nursing homes and hospitals while she makes her rounds. When they visit people's homes, he stays in the car or takes a walk. Once an old lady whose invalid sister is among Angela's regular communicants spots him standing beside the car in front of her house. "Would your companion like to come in?" she asks.

For a moment Angela doesn't know what the old lady's talking about. "Oh, that's Forrest, my husband," she says. "No, he's all right. Really, he prefers to wait outside."

"I just thought he looked cold," the woman says.

"That's very kind of you. But the truth is, he's not a Catholic. The rituals make him a little uncomfortable."

"What a shame. And yet he drove you here. That's good of him! You tell him next time he can come in the kitchen and sit with a cup of tea. He doesn't have to bother with the rest of it if he doesn't want to."

"I'll tell him." She doesn't though; it would make her self-conscious having Forrest around while she performs her sacramental duties. Is that wrong? she wonders. To exclude him from a possible occasion of grace because it's easier for her?

"Do you ever think you'd like to go with me into the sick people's rooms?" she asks him.

"Why would I want to do that?"

"No reason. I didn't think you did."

"One saint in the family's enough," he says.

If only he knew how unlike a saint she feels. How little charity is in her heart when she ministers to the dying; how much pity and fear is there instead. But he's not the most observant or sympathetic man. Nor can she detect in him any consciousness of his own mortality. He seems to regard these trips they take together around the city as a kind of lark. Angela, meanwhile, offers them up as penance, hoping to shorten her soul's stay in purgatory. Purgatory—that middling state where she most often pictures herself in the afterlife—seems such an inevitable stop along the way to eternity she can't understand the Protestants' refusal to believe in it. It's the sort of place Angela can almost imagine getting to by bus or train. Heaven and hell, by contrast, seem rather far-off and fanciful destinations, and when she tries to think about them very hard her faith wavers. She cannot traverse the vast spaces involved. Maybe her spiritual wings have been clipped by living too long with a skeptic; sometimes she believes so.

ONE DAY FORREST pulls into a taco place for lunch. "This kind of food doesn't agree with me," Angela informs him.

"You should try new things."

But the burrito she orders utterly defeats her attempts to eat it. Every time she picks the thing up something falls out. She ends up sawing at it with a plastic knife and fork, while Forrest watches, a big, silly grin on his face. "It won't be so funny if this makes me sick," she says.

"Alton loves this stuff." He eyes his own order suspiciously.

"Heaven knows why. It's not how I raised him."

"That's probably why."

She looks at him. Sometimes his acuteness surprises her. "I guess that's right," she says.

The restaurant is full of boys belching at each other and girls swinging their hair around. There's a high school down the road and they must come here for lunch. At first Angela feels conspicuous—they're the only old people—but none of the kids pay them any mind. We're invisible to them, she realizes.

Forrest seems to have caught a certain friskiness in the teenagers' manner. He reaches across the table, spears part of the burrito with her plastic fork, and tries feeding it to her. She gives him a look like "What do you think you're doing?" and he relinquishes the fork.

What is *she* doing here, in this unlikely place, with this unlikely man, on her way to visit yet another deathbed? The breathtaking conviction sweeps over her that it's all wrong somehow—ridiculous and accidental. Her son and daughter don't need her anymore. The sick people she visits don't need her; not really. If she didn't tend to them someone else would, and probably more effectively, or at least in a more cheerful spirit. And what of Forrest and her? What had that old lady called him? Her companion. Quaint phrase. But were there ever two people more ill-matched? Yet he imagines he'd like to travel halfway around the world with her. What would they think to talk about once they were alone under those palm trees he dreams of?

"Forrest, what did you ever see in me?" she asks.

"That's tough."

"Try anyway."

"Let me think. You had a funny way of walking."

"That's not true. I was the most poised of my sisters. The three of us used to go around the house with books on our heads. Do you believe we actually did that?"

"You didn't have any book on your head the time I'm thinking of. You were walking across Volker Park, going very fast, with your head down. It looked like you might bump into something and never know what it was."

"I was in a hurry, I guess."

"So what else is new?"

"Okay, you saw me in the park. Is that all?"

He flushes slightly. "I wished you'd look up."

"At you, you mean? This is before we met, I take it."

"Must have been."

"Did you ever tell me that before?" she says.

"Sure."

"I don't remember it."

"I do."

SISSY CALLS TO let them know she'll be out of the country for a few days; she's going to Cancun with her new boyfriend, the land developer.

"How well do you know this person?" Angela asks her daughter.

"What do you mean?"

"I mean, in a foreign country like that, you'll be completely at this man's mercy. Are you sure you can trust him?"

"What do you think he's going to do to me, Mother?"

"Sissy knows how to take care of herself," Forrest puts in.

"Ha!" Angela says.

Her daughter's voice comes to her across the miles with cold formality: "I just called to let you know where I was going. As a courtesy."

"Have a good time, honey," Forrest says.

"Doesn't it bother you, her going off with some man?" Angela asks after they hang up.

Forrest pretends to ignore the question, puckering up in one of his silent whistles and staring off into a corner.

"I think it's trampish," she says. "And don't tell me times have changed. Or she's in love. That doesn't make it right."

"I wouldn't try to tell you anything, Angela."

"It doesn't show much consideration for her father, is all I can say. Not three weeks ago she told you she was too busy to take a trip. But she can find time to go off with this ... this stranger whose name we don't even know. Forrest, we don't even know his name!"

"Joe, it's Joe ... something. Hell, Angela, will you relax?"

"What if there's an emergency and we need to get in touch with her?"

After she makes him call Sissy back to get the boyfriend's full name and address, as well as the address and phone number of the place where they'll be staying, she begins to feel bad about what she said to Forrest, about how his daughter would rather go off with her boyfriend than him. She knows why she said it: his unruffled manner in troubled circumstances never reflects even a fraction of her own anxiety, and this apparent unconcern on his part makes her lash out at him. Still, it was a mean thing for her to do. "You know what that girl's problem with men is?" she says to him later, under the guise of enumerating Sissy's faults. "She can never find one she loves and respects as much as her father. And that's the truth. I give this Joe person about six months. Tops."

MR. WETZEL RINGS up to request that Angela bring Communion to his wife again. "I think she's ready now." He speaks almost in a whisper. "She hasn't got long." Then he's weeping, but softly so his wife won't hear. Angela says maybe the priest should see her, but Mr. Wetzel says, no, his wife never had any use for that priest. Angela believes it; she's heard the priest on the subject of Greta Wetzel. Angela agrees to come first thing in the morning. "I'm dreading this one," she confides to Forrest.

She has a hard time sleeping that night; it's like a weight is pressing down on her chest. She has to prop herself up with pillows just to get a good, deep breath. Forrest sleeps flat on his back, without even a pillow, his hands folded on his stomach. Except for the steady rise and fall of his breathing, he might be posing as his own corpse. Where does he travel in his sleep? she wonders. Down what tree-lined boulevard, village lane, or mountain pass? Is she with him? Does he take her hand and say, "Do you know where you are now? Do you?" Or has she forfeited that privilege? Watching him, she feels abandoned, left behind, balked at the beginning of some journey she hasn't the courage to undertake.

In the morning when they get up, everything outside is covered with ice. "Just look at it!" Forrest says. "The paper never said anything about this."

"It's like something out of a fairy tale." Angela's thinking, a reprieve, a dispensation! No visit to Greta Wetzel's, after all. Not today. Maybe never. Who knows, by the time the streets are passable ... She won't allow herself to complete the thought, not only because it's a terrible one but because it might break the spell, cause time to lurch forward again; the sun might come out and the weather start to thaw. She holds her breath, listening to the crystalline trees brushing against the roof and windows.

Down in the kitchen she feels inspired to make a big breakfast. She's ravenous. "Forrest," she calls, "would you like bacon or sausage with your waffles? Or both? Forrest?" Now what's he up to?

Was that the front door she heard open and close a minute ago? When he finally appears in the kitchen, huffing and puffing, his face looks red enough to melt ice. "Your breakfast is cold," she informs him.

"I got the chains on the car."

"What on earth for?"

"You've got an appointment, right?"

"Forrest, are you crazy? No one will expect us in this weather."

"I thought you'd be dressed by now," he says.

"Did you really put the chains on the car?"

"Yes. The engine's running. Let's go."

"I'm going to call Mr. Wetzel right now and say we can't make it."

"We can make it, Angela. I can go anywhere with those chains."

She wants to say, "Why are you doing this to me? You're not even the one whose job it is." But all that comes out is, "Forrest, if we end up in a ditch somewhere!"

"Take baby steps," he advises her, as they shuffle side-by-side down the walk to the waiting car. On the front seat is a brochure open to a picture of a beach with sun-swept dunes in the foreground and a lavender sea shimmering behind. "Cute," she says. "Very funny."

He's right about the chains getting them through though. They work like a charm, and it helps that no one else is on the road. Forrest, she reminds herself, usually knows what he's doing.

"Mr. Wetzel will certainly be surprised to see me." Her anxiety about braving both the weather and Greta Wetzel has begun to be tempered with a sense of virtue that she's doing this thing at all.

"Forrest, would you really like to go off somewhere like this?" She means like the beach in the brochure.

"Yes, I would."

"Don't look at me, please, look at the road."

"Okay. Are you having second thoughts about flying?"

Flying? Her heart sinks. She had wanted to say something to make him happy, to reward him for his faithful service of driving. She'd forgotten about the flying part. To be loosed from the earth! To put her life in the hands of unseen others! No, she couldn't do that. "What about the pill you mentioned?" she says. "Does it really knock you out?"

"Sure. Or hypnosis is even better. No side effects."

"You're kidding about hypnosis."

"Why?"

"Please-look-at-the-road-Forrest."

"It doesn't even take an expert. I could probably hypnotize you myself."

"You could not. I'd laugh in your face."

"You'd have to cooperate. You'd have to be in the right frame of mind."

Angela's not sure she possesses the right frame of mind to relinquish her conscious will to Forrest. "Anyway, we'll see," she says.

They come to a steep hill that leads up to the Wetzels' house. Angela imagines sour Greta Wetzel waiting for her at the top of the glassy incline, like a damsel in a storybook who, deep down, wants to be rescued but, in her perversity, is compelled to invent obstacles. Angela says a prayer for the woman, that she will be open to grace, then says one for herself, that she'll make it through this. But she forgets to pray for the car. It starts to slip on the road; the car fishtails.

"Forrest!"

Just then, the chains catch—Angela can feel them taking hold. She can actually feel it in her chest, as if a string around her heart has suddenly been pulled taut and is drawing her onward. "Up we go," Forrest says. The car is at such a tilt all she can see is the sky.